Olive's
Ocean

KEVIN HENKES

Olive's Ocean

Greenwillow Books
An Imprint of HarperCollins*Publishers*

Printed in the United States of America. For information, address HarperCollins Children's Books, a division of HarperCollins Publishers, 1350 Avenue of the Americas, New York, NY 10019. www.harperchildrens.com

The text of this book is set in 11-point Bell.

This book is printed on acid-free paper.

Library of Congress Cataloging-in-Publication Data

Henkes, Kevin.

Olive's ocean / by Kevin Henkes.

   p.   cm.

"Greenwillow Books."

Summary: On a summer visit to her grandmother's cottage by the ocean, twelve-year-old Martha gains perspective on the death of a classmate, on her relationship with her grandmother, on her feelings for an older boy, and on her plans to be a writer.

ISBN 0-06-053543-1 (trade). ISBN 0-06-053544-X (lib. bdg.)

[1. Grandmothers—Fiction. 2. Family life—Fiction. 3. Self-perception—Fiction.] I. Title.

   PZ7.H389 Ol 2003 [Fic]—dc21   2002029782

10 9 8 7

First Edition

For Susan

1

A Beginning

"Are you Martha Boyle?"

Martha nodded.

"You don't know me," said the woman at the door. "Olive Barstow was my daughter. I was her mother."

Martha heard herself gasp. A small, barely audible gasp.

"I don't know how well you knew Olive," said the woman. "She was so shy." The woman reached into the pocket of the odd smock she was wearing and retrieved a folded piece of paper. "But I found this in her journal, and I think she'd want you to have it."

The rusted screen that separated them gave the woman a gauzy appearance. Martha cracked open the door to receive the pink rectangle.

"That's all," the woman said, already stepping off the stoop. "And thank you. Thank you, Martha Boyle."

The woman mounted a very old bicycle and

pedaled away, her long, sleek braid hanging behind her like a tail.

Breathing deeply to quiet her heart, Martha remained by the door thinking about Olive Barstow, unable for the moment to unfold the paper and read it.

2
An End

Olive Barstow was dead. She'd been hit by a car on Monroe Street while riding her bicycle. Weeks ago. That was about all Martha knew.

A sad image of Olive rose in Martha's mind: a quiet, unremarkable girl, a loner with averted eyes, clinging to the lockers when walking down the hallways at school.

The image that flashed next was imagined and worse: Olive flying through the air, after impact, like a bird, then scraping along the pavement and lying in a heap at the curbside, never to move again.

3
Hopes

Slowly, Martha unfolded the piece of paper. Olive's handwriting was perfectly formed—small, dense, controlled—like rows and rows of pearls. Martha read, hearing the words in Olive's thin, hesitant voice.

June 7: My Hopes

I hope that I can write a book someday. Not like the kind we did in writing lab. A real one, like in a library or bookstore. And not a mystery or adventure one, but an emotional one. Maybe I can make kids change their opinions on emotion books like some authors did to me. Most kids at school call the kind of book I want to do a chapter book, but I call them novels. Maybe I could be the youngest person ever to write a novel. Maybe I can develop a unique style of writing that no other authors have. I already know the first sentence of my novel: "The orphan's secret wish was that her bones were hollow like a bird's and that she could just take off and fly away."

I also hope that one day I can go to a real ocean such as the Atlantic or Pacific. I like Madison with all the lakes (especially Lake Wingra), but I think it is not the same. When I'm eighteen I want to live in a cottage on a cliff that looks over the sea.

What else do I hope?

I hope that I get to know Martha Boyle next year (or this summer). I hope that we can be friends. That is my biggest hope. She is the nicest person in my whole entire class.

An eerie feeling invaded Martha's body. She was holding a piece of paper that had come from the journal of someone her own age, someone now dead. But there was more. Martha would be leaving with her family the next morning to visit her grandmother at her grandmother's house on the Atlantic Ocean (Martha's favorite place in the world). Also, she had recently decided that she was going to be a writer—and this was still such a private thought that she hadn't even told her best friend, or her brother, or her parents. And, what, she wondered, had she ever done or said to Olive Barstow that would compel her to write that Martha was "the nicest person in my whole entire class"? Most eerie—she would never know the answer.

Minutes earlier, she had been packing her bags for vacation, feeling completely happy, and now she felt different—altered. The longer Martha mulled over the coincidences, the more startling they became.

4
Martha's Father

"Who was at the door?" asked Dennis Boyle, Martha's father. "You look like you've seen a ghost."

"Oh, no one," Martha replied, shrugging. "Just someone for me. Nothing, really." She folded the paper and hid it in her palm. "Really. Nothing. No one."

"Well, that surely clears things up," said her father. He tipped his head and half smiled. His expression was hard for Martha to interpret; she read it as: I love you, but I don't understand you.

"Listen," her father continued, "I need your help. Lucy's still napping, and I have to go to the store to get a few new things—toys, books, whatever—to keep her occupied on the airplane tomorrow. I need you to watch her when she wakes up."

"Sure," said Martha.

"Your mother should be home soon. And Vince is at Robbie's house. If anyone asks about dinner, tell them I said it's a carryout night. Too much to do before we leave for Godbee's." He was holding a laundry basket heaped high with all sorts of things: clothes, newspapers, a rubber ball, dirty dishes, CDs, bottles of sunscreen, Lucy's plastic sandals. "This basket represents my life," he said in a slightly numbed tone, placing the basket solidly on the coffee table. "I'll be back."

And he was gone.

The summer seemed to be taking its toll on Martha's father. Whenever possible, he found an excuse to escape from the house by himself. He admitted that he was looking forward to the end of summer and the beginning of school; Martha and her older brother, Vince, would be away most of the day, of course, and Lucy would be going to nursery school three mornings a week.

It was the middle of August. After Martha and her family returned from their vacation, there would be just one week for her father to get through before he'd have more time alone.

Dennis Boyle had quit his job as a lawyer when Lucy was born and had been taking care of her full-time for the past two and a half years. He also had been trying to write a novel during this time, although no one in the family had read a word. Periodically, and with growing frequency, his face was darkened by thought. "The novel," he'd say. "I'm thinking about my novel."

Martha hadn't told anyone about her decision to be a writer yet, mostly because she didn't want her father to think she was copying him. But she had given herself a deadline—she would tell him before they came back home from Godbee's.

5
Lucy

In her bedroom, leaning into the wall, Martha started punching the buttons on the telephone automatically. She was calling her best friend, Holly, to tell her about Olive Barstow's mother and the journal page, but stopped before the last digit and switched the phone off. She wasn't ready.

After slipping the folded journal page into one of the side zippered compartments of her backpack, Martha walked to Lucy's room. She tried to be as quiet as possible. Lucy was such a light sleeper that stepping on a creaky floorboard or speaking in a normal voice near her could easily rouse her. "I breathe too loudly and she wakes up," their father had often complained. "Other people's kids sleep through train wrecks."

From the door frame, Martha peeked at her sister. Lucy slept on a queen-size mattress on the floor that took up most of the room. The window shade was pulled, the room shadowy.

It was almost like a game or puzzle to find Lucy—she was curled up against a pillow and nearly hidden by five other pillows, her quilt, a sheet, and dozens of stuffed animals and dolls. One doll in particular was Lucy's match in size and hair color. More than once, in a similar situation—in bed, in the dark—Martha had, for an instant, confused the two.

Martha couldn't shake Olive Barstow from her thoughts. She felt a stab of loneliness, the source of which she couldn't name. She cleared her throat, first softly, and then noisily. She coughed.

Lucy rustled, twisting herself into the sheet. Her eyes flew open. Blinked. Like a fish surfacing, she seemed to be quickly making her way through layers, from sleep to wakefulness.

"Lucy-poo," Martha sang. "Oh, Lucy-poo." Martha lay down beside her baby sister and nibbled at her soft pink ear.

Lucy's head popped up. "I wake up," she chirped.

"You did and I'm glad," said Martha, twirling and twirling a strand of her sister's curly red hair. "You are the most beautiful baby in the world."

"I *two*," Lucy said emphatically. With a bounce, she rose to her feet, holding both hands, ten fingers splayed. "Two."

"Almost three," said Martha. "And how old am I?"

"Two."

"No, I'm twelve. Say twelve."

"Telve," Lucy replied, cocking her head and beaming.

"I need to change your diaper," Martha said, scooping up her sister and squeezing her, "and then I'll take you for a ride in your stroller."

"Two," said Lucy.

6

The Corner of
Knickerbocker and Monroe

Because she had a purpose, Martha walked briskly, pushing Lucy's stroller through the neighborhood. The sun was hidden by clouds, then in full view, then blocked by trees or a house, then in full view again, so that it felt to Martha as if she were passing through a series of rooms, each room lit differently. It was very hot, and the humidity was high. One house they passed on Fox Avenue had beach towels draped over the front bushes to dry, reminding Martha that she hadn't packed her beach towel yet, or her bathing suit. What else had she forgotten? She felt scattered. There was a break in the sidewalk that Martha hadn't noticed; the stroller lurched.

"Sorry," said Martha.

"Eeeee," Lucy squealed, thrilled by the bump and the speed. She giggled.

They kept going—turning corners, following curving streets.

Martha stopped. This was the spot. The

corner of Knickerbocker and Monroe. Lake Wingra glistened in the distance.

There was nothing to indicate that this was the site of a tragedy. There were no bouquets or teddy bears piled along the curbside. No ribbons laced through the nearby fence.

And now that Martha had arrived at her destination, she wondered what to do next. Why had she decided to come here? What had she expected would happen? She licked her upper lip thoughtfully.

"Go, go," Lucy demanded, waving her arms and kicking.

"Just a minute," said Martha. She pushed the stroller ahead a few inches, then pulled it back. She repeated the movement—lifting the front wheels off the ground every second or third time—with the hope that the motion, the rhythm, would keep Lucy content.

Martha watched the cars coming from both directions on Monroe Street, her eyes flicking back and forth. She tried to imagine what it would feel like to be hit by a car. Keeping one hand on the stroller at all times, Martha turned it away from the traffic and placed her left foot in the street. A mail truck sounded its horn as it thundered past, and Martha could feel its power. The force blew her hair away from her face. She winced; even her toes tightened.

Lucy started to fuss, crowning her little diatribe with a piercing noise—her injured bird cry, as their father referred to it.

"Okay," said Martha. "We'll go." And then a thought occurred to her. Attached to the back of the stroller was a canvas pouch that held small toys and snacks for Lucy. At the bottom of the pouch, among the trinkets, crayons, and cracker crumbs, Martha searched for a piece of sidewalk chalk. Found one. Blue. Quickly she stepped back and wrote the word OLIVE on the top of the curb in broad capital letters. Then, instinctively, she unhooked the bracelet from her wrist and coiled it inside the letter O. Martha had made the bracelet herself. The colors of the beads changed from yellow to orange to red to purple to blue to green and back to yellow, like a rainbow.

"Go!" Lucy yelled. "Go!"

"All right," said Martha. "Calm down."

"Where we go?" asked Lucy as they headed back up Knickerbocker Street.

"We go home," said Martha, unaware that she sounded just like her two-year-old sister. And unaware that, even as she steered the stroller, she was still clutching the chalk and it was turning her hand blue.

7

A Phone Conversation in Mid-July

"Hello?"

"Holly, it's me."

"Just a minute. I'm getting some M&M's. Okay."

"Did you hear about Olive Barstow?"

"Yeah. Oh, my God. Can you believe it?"

"It's so awful. My mom told me. She passed the accident on her way to work this morning. She called from her office to ask if I knew her."

"Josh Sweeney told me. He said she wasn't wearing a helmet and that her head came off and that her blood wasn't red, but black."

"That's not true. Josh Sweeney is the biggest idiot-scuzzbag-jerk-of-the-world. I don't know how you can live next door to him." Pause. "He was so mean to her. So was Dana Lewis."

"I know." Pause. "I hate crossing Monroe Street."

"I know." Pause. "I feel so bad. I mean, we should have been nicer to her."

"Martha, we *were* nice." Pause. *Crunch, crunch.* "We weren't *not* nice."

"I know, but we should have asked her to sit at our table at lunch, or at least talked to her more, or something."

"She was kind of . . . I mean . . . *weird.*"

"Don't say that about a dead person."

"Well, she was. Sort of."

"She was nice. She was quiet."

"I guess."

"I don't think she had any friends." Pause. "It would be awful not to have friends."

Silence.

Crunch, crunch.

Silence.

"Martha Boyle, you think too much. And my dad says when you think too much, that's when the trouble starts." Pause. "He mostly says it to my mom."

Silence.

"Hey, Martha, do you want to go shopping on State Street? I'll see if my mom will take us. Maybe we can have lunch, too. At the food carts."

"I don't know."

"Sticky rice with mangoes?"

"Maybe."

"See if you can, and call me back."

"Okay."

"Bye."

"Bye."

8

Ms. Hubbard

"Did you listen to my show today?"

Olive Barstow had joined Martha's class very late in the school year. Right before Valentine's Day. School had ended during the first week of June.

"The woman I interviewed was wonderful. An eighty-eight-year-old scuba diver."

The accident that killed Olive had happened in the middle of July.

"Do you want to hear about her?"

Olive's mother delivered the page from the journal in the middle of August—just hours earlier.

"I'll take that as a yes."

Martha's mother, Alice Hubbard, sat down on the edge of Martha's bed. Martha was sitting on the bed already. A small suitcase, half packed, lay open between them.

"She's exactly what I want to be like when I'm eighty-eight," said Martha's mother. She plucked a T-shirt from the suitcase, refolded it, gently replaced it, then smoothed it with both hands. She raised her eyebrows and widened her eyes—cocked her head, too—inviting her daughter to speak.

Martha scrunched up her face. "I feel a little spacey. Sorry." She had been trying to piece together the facts about Olive Barstow, the outline of Olive's life for the short time it had intersected with her own. Martha realized how little she knew. For the most part Olive was a mystery.

Martha knew nothing about Olive's home life, nothing about her family, except that her mother rode a bike and wore her hair in a braid. Olive's school life, from Martha's perspective, didn't offer many answers either. Olive had seemed nearly invisible, passing through the halls and days unnoticed, except when she was being teased by Josh Sweeney or Dana Lewis.

"I can tell I'm boring you," said Martha's mother. She'd risen from the bed and was walking away. A muscle in her cheek moved. "I'll leave you alone."

"Whatever," said Martha. "I mean, you don't have to," she added, trying to soften the sharpness of her response.

"I'll call you when dinner gets here." Her

mother's voice came from the hallway.

"Is Vince home yet?"

This time it was Martha's question left unanswered. Either her mother hadn't heard it, or she was ignoring Martha to get back at her just a little.

Lately they'd been annoying each other, rubbing each other the wrong way.

Alice Hubbard worked for Wisconsin Public Radio. She produced and hosted a radio talk show that aired every weekday morning. It was rebroadcast at night and syndicated nationally. What used to provide a sense of pride for Martha ("You're really on the radio, Mama!" "People in New York *and* California *and* Florida hear you every day!") had, as she'd gotten older, become a source of embarrassment ("I can't believe you said the word crotch for the whole world to hear. I'll never be able to show my face at school again." "Your laugh is so . . . gross, Mom. Can't you just not laugh? Please? If you love me at all.").

Sometimes, when Martha was irritated with her mother, or felt ignored by her, she called her Ms. Hubbard under her breath, rather than Mom. Sometimes, Martha's feelings for her mother bounced between love and hate quickly and without warning, as if her feelings were illogical, willful, and completely out of Martha's control.

Suddenly Martha's bed felt huge and empty without her mother sitting beside her. Martha wanted her mother to come back so she could tell her about Olive. She wanted to curl up with her mother the way she used to when she was younger and life was uncomplicated.

In a second, sadness and longing turned to grumpiness and anger.

"Thanks for your help, Ms. Hubbard," she said.

9

Vince

Martha's brother, Vince, was one year older than she. Exactly. Martha was born on Vince's first birthday. "I'm the best present you'll ever get," Martha used to like to say. She rarely said it anymore, even on their birthday.

Besides a birthday, they had shared a room—until Martha was in third grade and Vince was in fourth. It was Vince who finally wanted a room of his own, claiming he despised girls. But Martha wouldn't budge, and so it was Vince who had to move out.

Martha never believed his pronouncement, and as proof that her opinion was accurate, Vince started coming to her room nearly every night to talk before he went to bed—and still did years later. Some nights they talked for a half hour, others less than a minute. Even when they were at war with each other, he'd make a brief appearance at her door.

"You're an absolute jerk," he might yell.

"Goes double for you," she'd yell back.

"If you get any uglier, we'll have to remove all the mirrors in the house and paint all the windows and any other reflecting surfaces to save you from the horror."

That's when her door would slam and the entire house would quake.

Martha admired her brother, and liked and loved him, too, even as she sometimes was offended by him. He was sarcastic and funny and smart and oddly childlike, and could be counted on to be brutally honest concerning matters of the greatest importance. "You've got a zit on the back of your neck that's ready to explode," he'd once told her. "Don't wear those shoes in public," he'd said another time, "unless you want to look like a complete dork."

The thought struck her once and returned from time to time that, sadly, she would never catch up to him. He would always be just a little ahead of her. Forever.

Should she tell her brother about Olive Barstow? She wondered about this as she waited for him to show up. Her bags were packed and lined up by her dresser. She was on her bed, leafing through a magazine. She had already called her friend Holly to say good-bye, but she hadn't told her about Olive and had hung up quickly, not being in the mood for chatting.

"Hey," said Vince, galumphing into the room with his big clumsy feet and his friendly, rubbery face. He had so many freckles—tons of them everywhere. Acne camouflage. He even had them on his nostrils, eyelids, ears, and lips.

Martha felt as if an easy breeze had swept through the room. "Hi."

"I shaved for the first time today," Vince told her. He was leaning over the bed, his head coming right at her like a pitched ball.

"Really? You shaved?" She thought he was joking, but then noticed that his skin looked irritated along his jawline, pink and blotchy. She stifled a laugh. "Why? You didn't need to."

"I'll admit," said Vince, retreating a bit, "it was mostly just peach fuzz."

Martha had scrutinized her face in the bathroom mirror enough to know that even she had fine fair hair all over. "*I've* got peach fuzz. Everyone's got peach fuzz. You don't shave peach fuzz."

"It was a little more than that," he said evenly, stroking his chin.

"Not much," she said. "Not like a man or anything."

He shrugged, then looked at her with narrow, narrow eyes. "I have to finish packing." He was leaving.

"Hey, Vince?" She was afraid she'd hurt his feelings. The last thing she'd intended to do.

"Huh?" He stopped but didn't turn around, his back facing her. His red hair spun out from the very center of his head, from a perfect white dot of scalp, an extra eye.

What could she say? Her lips were parted, open, as if her mouth had been frozen in midsentence. "Nothing."

"Gotta go," he mumbled.

She was alone again. "Night," she said to her pillow.

In a moment of self-pity, Martha felt as if everyone were abandoning her. She felt hollowed out, except for her brain, which was full and racing.

With the light off, her room played tricks on her; the walls seemed very close, then far away. Martha tried to empty her mind, make it a bare room, stripped clean. But *she* kept creeping back. Olive.

It seemed like forever that Martha lay awake. It was thinking of the ocean, remembering it, its endlessness, that finally allowed her to fall asleep.

10
Airplane

While riding on the airplane, in the middle of the flight, Martha tried to compose something—anything—holding her notebook close to her chest, so that no one could read what she was writing.

Nearly an hour later, as the airplane began its descent into Providence, Martha closed her notebook and replaced it in her backpack. She had only written two words: *Olive Barstow.*

11
The Glittery Feeling

They were outside, at the airport, waiting for the shuttle bus to take them to the car-rental lot. Martha thought she smelled the ocean already and was immediately excited. She breathed deeply, letting the feeling sink in. They would be at Godbee's shortly, right on the water, and every molecule, every atom, knew it.

She called the feeling the glittery feeling, and she always experienced it when they were this close, when they were at this part of their trip to Godbee's.

The glittery feeling. She'd named it because it felt to her as if her skin and everything beneath it briefly became shiny and jumpy and bubbly, as if glitter materialized inside her, then rose quickly through the layers of tissue that comprised her, momentarily sparkling all over the surface of her skin before dissipating into the air.

Martha closed her eyes and let her arms

drift slightly upward. She couldn't help her-self. A small joyful squeak escaped from her throat.

"What do you think you are? A bird?" It was Vince.

Her arms fell.

"The bus is here," said her father. "Grab everything and hurry."

Her mother accidentally bumped her with a suitcase as they jockeyed for a place on the curb among the crowd. "*Move*, honey," she said.

The glittery feeling was gone.

12
Godbee

The sky was full—of blue and sun. The ocean reflected it and was flat and glossy like a fancy ballroom floor. To Martha, this was the most beautiful sight, a miracle. The ocean made her feel insignificant and slightly afraid, but in an exhilarating way. Her inclination was not to walk or dance across the water's surface. Nor to swim through it. She wanted to _be_ the ocean.

"I love it here, Godbee," Martha said to her grandmother.

"I do, too," replied Dorothy Boyle. "Especially with you here." Her voice was strong and even, belying her eighty-two years.

They were looking out onto Buzzard's Bay, sitting side-by-side on the old seawall in matching Adirondack chairs made by Martha's grandfather, who had died long before Martha was born. Godbee's house was directly behind them, a cedar-shingled cottage the color of brushed nickel.

Martha had come up with the nickname Godbee by accident when she was younger than Lucy. Dorothy Boyle had been referred to as Grandma Boyle or Grandma B, for short, to distinguish her from Martha's other grandmother, Anne Hubbard. As a toddler, Martha couldn't pronounce Grandma B correctly, or had misheard it, and had, for as long as she could remember, called her favorite grandmother Godbee. For some reason, it had caught on. Not only with everyone in Martha's family, but with some of Godbee's friends and neighbors, too.

"Stay by me for a bit, will you?" said Godbee. "Don't go running off like your brother and sister."

Martha smiled and nodded.

Vince had already disappeared from sight, having gone to look for his friends, the Mannings, who lived down the beach. There were five Manning brothers ranging in age from nine to fourteen. Despite the fact that Vince only saw them once or twice a year, he always fell back into their circle with great ease.

Martha's opinion of the Mannings had

changed over the years. She had liked them, ignored them, tolerated them, disliked them, hated them, and now found herself interested in seeing them, particularly Tate, who was thirteen, closest to her in age. She wondered what he looked like this year, how he had changed since last August.

Lucy was still within earshot, but barely. The seaweed strewn about the tideline had captured her attention. She poked at the stringy clumps with a stick. "Ribbons!" Martha heard her shriek. "Brown ribbons!" Their mother was following Lucy like a shadow, never more than a few steps back.

"Where did Dad go?" Martha wondered aloud.

"He's probably snooping through my drawers and medicine cabinet," said Godbee. "It's what he always does. It's annoying, but it's the duty of a good son. One day you'll worry about *your* parents the same way. Hard to believe, but the day will come."

A lone herring gull seemed to drop from the sky. It righted itself just before it struck the water. Squawking harshly, it rose again, dipped once, then glided directly over Martha, close enough to make her flinch.

"You've only been here a few hours," Godbee continued, "and already your father has asked enough questions about me and my body to fill the sea. When I'm here alone, I admit, I think about me, but now I want to think about you."

"Me?"

"You."

Martha shrugged. "I could tell you funny Lucy stories."

"No," said Godbee. "Tell me something about *you.*"

Martha shrugged again, keeping her shoulders up around her neck. "There's nothing to tell."

"I don't believe that for a minute."

"Lucy's more interesting," said Martha. "And Vince—" She didn't think she could finish the sentence and have it make sense to her grandmother. —is older? —is the oldest? —is always first? "—is Vince."

"Lucy is too young for me to really know," said Godbee. "And Vincent is a bit distant already, starting to move away."

What is she going to say about *me?* thought

Martha. But Godbee had stopped talking. Martha didn't know if it was her turn to speak or not. A pouty cry from Lucy carried in the open air, filling the silence.

"I have an idea," Godbee said suddenly. "You have to tell me something about yourself each day you're here. Something I don't know." She paused. "And, to make it fair," she added, "I'll do the same for you. What do you say?"

"I guess." How could she disappoint her favorite grandmother?

"Good," said Godbee. "Who knows, this might be our last summer together." And then her eyes strayed and fluttered shut, and she tilted her head to take full advantage of the sun.

13
Just Fine

Godbee's eyes were large and penetrating, icy gray. They were aimed right at Martha. "I'm not mad at you, darling," said Godbee. "And I had no intention of worrying you. It's just that at my age, one can't predict much of anything." She cleared her throat quietly. "I hadn't meant to sound cryptic."

Martha received the words in silence. Her face was serious and was partly turned away from her grandmother. Feelings, including great relief, rushed inside her. She managed a shy smile. "I didn't know Dad would lecture you," Martha finally said.

"I can take it. Now, smile a real smile for me so I know you're not suffering inside."

Martha complied, with some effort.

Although it had been delivered in a purely tranquil voice, her grandmother's comment had frightened her. *"Who knows, this might be our last summer together."* And so Martha had gotten her father alone and told him and asked the awful question: "Is Godbee dying?"

Her father, in turn, had confronted Godbee in the kitchen, closing the door behind them. Martha heard only murmuring. Her grandmother's side of the mumbled discourse sounded melodic, her father's reproving. She couldn't make out any actual words until her father flung the door wide open.

"She's twelve," said Martha's father, walking away from the discussion, "what do you *think* she'd think? What would *any*body think?" As he brushed past Martha, he added, "Your grandmother's just fine." He pronounced "just fine" so sharply, the words seemed to slash the air.

Godbee didn't seem fazed one bit. She flicked her hand at her son as if she were shooing a fly. But Martha felt responsible for her father's mood, a mood that hung over the house like a dark cloud.

"He's never been good at vacations," said Godbee. "Even when he was a boy."

His mood didn't improve at dinner; Lucy threw a full-fledged tantrum because they had no banana baby food for her to eat.

"I want bananas!"

"Damn," said her father. "We used the last jar on the plane."

"Didn't you pack extras?" asked Martha's mother.

"I can't always think of everything," her father snapped back, a crack of anger in his voice.

"There are bananas on the counter," said Godbee. "I'll mash one up."

"Forget it, Mom. She won't eat it."

Lucy was a picky eater. Banana baby food was one thing she currently liked.

"Bananas!" Lucy screamed. "I want bananas!" She was rocking back and forth in her chair, which was piled with books so that she could reach the table. Her face grew redder and redder. Her lips formed ugly shapes. Tears streamed down her cheeks. "Bananabanana-banana!"

"Stop it!" her father commanded, pounding the table. "I said STOP IT!"

The tiny kitchen shook. Something clattered.

Lucy became so hysterical, her jerky movements shifted the stack of books she was perched on, and she and the books tumbled from the chair. She kicked one of the table legs. She flung her arms about.

In an instant, Martha's mother was on the floor cradling Lucy, her arms circling Lucy's wriggling body, massaging it, as if by doing so the rage would be absorbed, transferred from daughter to mother.

"We're definitely on vacation now," said Vince. "I can feel every muscle relaxing. Who needs meditation when you can be with the Boyles? Even my baby toenails are relaxing."

Martha looked around the room. She hated everyone except Godbee. She hated Lucy for being so fussy. She hated her father for losing his temper. She hated Vince for being sarcastic in front of Godbee. She hated her mother for not fixing everything. Wasn't a mother supposed to fix everything? Make everything perfect?

Lucy quieted. She was whimpering now. And hiccuping. "I happy now," she moaned between two great heaves of her chest.

"I'll go to the store as soon as she's completely calmed down," said Martha's mother. "I can take her with me."

"No, I'm going," said Martha's father. "I'm

going alone. I'm going right now. I'm gone."

After the door slammed and a moment of awkward stillness, there was a moment of giddiness in which Martha giggled silently and Vince twirled his spoon, smirking, and Lucy squeaked gleefully, "Where's Papa? Where he hiding?" And then it was as if nothing at all out of the ordinary had happened.

"Please pass the salt, Vincent," said Godbee. "This soup is a bit bland."

14
Parcheesi

Martha's father didn't return and didn't return. And Martha started to worry.

No one else seemed concerned. Vince had gone over to the Mannings' to spend the night. Martha's mother and Lucy were together in the big upstairs bedroom, most likely sleeping by now, seeing as Martha didn't hear voices or footfalls coming from above any longer. (Lucy needed someone to lie with her until she fell asleep. "I'll be back in about fifteen minutes," Martha's mother had said. "I hope." But after forty-five minutes had passed, she still hadn't come back downstairs. She must have been exhausted from the trip, Martha thought. She's probably sleeping in her clothes.) And Godbee was humming intently as she and Martha played Parcheesi at the kitchen table. While Martha's mind dipped and dove and toyed with the idea of her father never returning, Godbee's mind seemed completely focused on Parcheesi.

To hide her preoccupation, Martha leaned forward and tapped her teeth, faking interest, pretending to be forming a strategy.

Playing Parcheesi was something they did during every visit, usually every night. Martha wondered how many games had been played on this board, with these markers. The markers were wooden and worn, smooth as sea glass. They were darkened by time and use, and the dye had faded, too, so that the red pieces were a dirty pink color like a smudged pencil eraser, the yellow ones more gray than yellow.

Martha felt Vince's absence, too—with an ache. It was usually the three of them—Godbee, Vince, and Martha—who played together.

"Stay," Martha had said as Vince headed for the door on his way to the Mannings'. "Please."

He didn't break his stride, but turned his head toward his sister long enough to flash a characteristic grin and waggle his eyebrows. If his thoughts had been printed above his head, Martha imagined them reading: PARCHEESI?! I'M OUT OF HERE. YOU'RE ALL SO BORING.

The world was changing before Martha's very eyes, and she hated it.

"You're not concentrating," Godbee said.

Martha shrugged. How could she?

"Here," said Godbee. She scooped up the game board, folded it into a V, slid the markers and dice into the box, fitted the board on top, and replaced the lid.

Martha sucked her lips into her mouth so they disappeared.

"You don't want to play any more than Vincent did," said Godbee.

"That's not true."

"Shall we start?"

"Another game?" Martha was confused.

"No, sweetie," said Godbee. "Our agreement. Remember? Are you ready to tell me something about you? Or shall I go first?"

"I . . ." Martha began. "I . . ." And then she bleated out her secret thought: "I hate my family right now. Everyone." She could feel her heart beat with each word. And she was startled by her words, as if someone else had spoken them. "Everyone but you."

She couldn't believe what she was saying. She might very well hate her father, but her father was Godbee's son, Godbee's only child. "I'm sorry?" she added as a question in a very weak voice. She had to muster every pinch of willpower she had to keep from crying.

Godbee looked at her with a face that held in it nothing but sympathy. "I know," she said. "I know. Hard to believe, but I still remember what it's like."

Before Godbee could press her to explain or ask probing questions, Martha said, "Will you tell *me* something now?" Quick, please, hurry, before I bawl my eyes out.

"Do you want to know what I hate?" asked Godbee.

Martha nodded.

"One morning last year," said Godbee, "I woke up to the fact that I despised my hands. Truly despised them. I know I'm at a point in my life where I should accept everything, but look at them. They're like crabs—ugly, pink, crippled crabs."

Martha looked. Maybe Godbee was right. Her grandmother's hands rested on the table-top in crablike curls. They were thin speckled and knobby. Martha had never paid much attention to them before. They had always been her grandmother's hands—nothing more, nothing less.

"They're nice," Martha whispered.

"Oh, honey," said Godbee, "you don't have to say that." She flexed her fingers slowly as she spoke. "Can you believe that when I was young, an older boy I only vaguely knew once asked to draw my hands, he thought them so beautiful?"

He probably thought that more than your hands were beautiful, Martha wanted to say. "Did he? Draw them?" she asked.

"Well," said Godbee, "you know, I was so shy that when—" But that's as far as she got. Two orbs of light shone through the window. Their beams blazed up the wall and slid across the ceiling, interrupting her midsentence. Then they disappeared.

Headlights.

Martha drew a quick breath inward. "He's back," she said. She heard the car engine shut off, a car door slam. And she chided herself silently for worrying so much. Her father wasn't *that* kind of father. Her father was not the kind to disappear.

Her father entered the kitchen carrying

three grocery bags. "I've been all over the damn cape," he said, "and now we've got enough banana baby food for everyone."

If he had said the exact words in a different voice, Martha could easily have thought him angry, but his tone and manner were buoyant. His face glowed. Light danced in his eyes.

He dumped the contents of one of the bags onto the counter. More than a dozen little jars clinked and rolled. Miraculously, none broke.

"While I was driving around," he said, "I had a revelation. I've made a decision. A big one." He paused and looked from side to side. "Where's your mother?"

"She's upstairs," Martha replied. She was trying to decipher what it was about her father that looked different. There was something. She couldn't pinpoint it. "I think she's sleeping."

"Then I'll tell you two first. Test the waters."

15

Her Father's Decision

Martha drank in her father's words.

His news was only shocking to her because of the way in which it had changed him. She had figured it out: When he had left the house, his face was all sharp angles, and upon his return, his face had softened. His muscles, bones, features, were in repose, relaxed.

He had decided that he wanted to abandon his novel and go back to work full-time, either at the law firm he had worked at before or someplace, anyplace, else.

"What will Alice think?" Godbee asked.

For a second the sharp angles resurfaced, then settled again. "I think she'll be fine about it. The extra money won't hurt. I'll be much happier. That'll make everyone else happier."

The decision meant that Lucy would need more child care, but that had nothing to do with Martha. That was her parents' concern.

What the decision *did* mean for Martha was that now she was free to be the one and only writer in her family.

It was meant to be.

16

Kissing

On the first morning there was always the strangeness and excitement of waking up in a new place, a new bed. It was like living in a dream for a few minutes before realizing where you actually were and how you got there.

Some things stayed the same year after year: the sound of the ocean so close, the walls as yellow as a canary, the sea glass and jingle shells scattered across the windowsills like handfuls of confetti.

And there were always the same smells that combined in some way to make the one house smell that was Godbee's. When Martha tried to dissect the one house smell into its many parts, she could only come up with these: the kitchen sink smell, the fireplace smell, the smell of Godbee's hand lotion, and the smell of the damp bed sheets, which was sharp, of bleach. But there had to have been more, because the mixture of them all was such a good smell, one of the most comforting Martha knew.

And, of course, there was always the smell of the ocean, but that smell seemed separate to Martha, bigger.

Martha lingered in bed. She heard laughter from below. She sniffed once more, stretched like a cat, then went downstairs thinking, happily, I'm going to be a writer.

Lucy greeted Martha at the kitchen threshold with a hug. Martha stooped so that Lucy could give her a good-morning kiss. As was their routine, Lucy grabbed Martha's face, hands on cheeks, and gave her big sister a dramatic smooch. If Lucy didn't meet her sister's lips square on, she would declare the kiss a "bad one" and try again. Sometimes they had to try ten times before they got it exactly right and Lucy was satisfied.

"Good one," said Lucy on the first attempt.

"*Great* one," said Martha, rising.

"No," said Lucy, stamping her foot. "*Good* one!"

"Oh, right," said Martha. "Good one."

"Right," said Lucy.

It suddenly struck Martha that Lucy looked

like a peony in her ruffled pink bathing suit, and Martha laughed silently, the way an adult might.

"She's something," said Godbee. "Tiny, but mighty." Godbee made her way over to Martha, and, imitating Lucy, held Martha's face and kissed her.

"Good one," said Martha.

More kissing. Martha's parents were standing by the sink—kissing and smiling and kissing and laughing and kissing. If Vince had been around he would have said that his parents were exhibiting MSB. Morning Sex Behavior.

"When they do it in the morning," Vince had informed Martha earlier that summer during one of their nightly chats, "they're all giggly and kissy and weird for at least an hour afterward. It's unmistakable."

Martha blushed. She could feel warmth spread through her neck, cheeks, and ears.

Her parents snatched her up and kissed the top of her head. Enveloped, she forgot that she hated her family.

Martha broke free. "Did you tell Mom your news?" she asked her father.

"He did," said her mother.

"I did," said her father.

Martha didn't need to ask what her mother thought about her father's decision. The mood that filled the kitchen and the looks on her parents' faces gave away everything and were really all the information she needed.

"We're going for a walk to the harbor," said Martha's father. "Want to join us?" Even when he wasn't smiling, he appeared to be on the verge of doing so, an arsenal of buried smiles waiting just beneath the surface.

"Did you have breakfast already?" asked Martha.

Her parents nodded.

"I eated bananas," said Lucy. She placed her hands on her round belly and moved them in widening circles. "Bananas and bananas and bananas," she added, tossing her head from side to side.

"Maybe I'll stay here with Godbee," said Martha, "and have something to eat, too." She spotted a stack of dirty plates and bowls in the sink. "And help clean up."

But neither breakfast nor doing the dishes was foremost in her mind.

17

A Writer

With no ocean breeze, it was hot and stuffy in the kitchen. Sunlight poured through the windows, intensifying the heat. A fine sheen of perspiration had bloomed all over Martha's body. She stretched her tongue to lick the sweat off the cleft between her nose and upper lip.

Godbee had no air-conditioning, except for a small window unit in her bedroom. She had no dishwasher either. No e-mail. No computer. No portable telephone—just an ancient stationary one by the back door, with a cord like black curling ribbon. Life at Godbee's seemed old-fashioned to Martha. But the things Martha could not live without at home, she barely missed when she was at her grandmother's.

Martha had eaten; the dishes had just been finished.

"What should I do with these?" asked Martha. She held up one of the empty, washed baby food jars.

"I'll save them," said Godbee. "You never know, they might come in handy for something. Keep the lids, too. Just line them up under the window for me."

Martha did as instructed. Then she dried her hands on a dish towel so thin she could see through it. Looking at her own hands made her think of Godbee's withered ones, and Martha wondered what her grandmother would tell about herself next.

"Let's sit outside," said Godbee.

"I'll get dressed and meet you," replied Martha, glancing down at the large, bright orange T-shirt she wore as pajamas. It was her theory that, contrasted with bright orange, the color of her hair was less shocking, and so she had started wearing bright orange clothes. And she nearly always pulled her unruly hair back into a ponytail with an elastic band. If she didn't, it looked as if wild flames were circling her head, fanning out in every direction. Too conspicuous. Sometimes she doubted her theory, wondering if the orange called *more* attention to her hair. But then she doubted just about everything in her life anyway, and continued the practice.

When Martha returned and sat down outside next to her grandmother, she was wearing a different, clean, large, bright orange T-shirt (she owned four of them) over her bathing suit.

"You look the same, sweetie," said Godbee, who typically wore blousy floral-print dresses in pastel colors. "Your night clothes and day clothes are interchangeable."

"I guess."

"The modern world," said Godbee.

Martha decided to get right to the point. It was a new day, and she decided she wanted to get on with their agreement. By confiding in Godbee again, Martha thought she could at least partially erase the embarrassment of what she had said yesterday. She adjusted herself, straightened her shoulders, bracing herself for what she was about to say, what she had not yet told anyone. "I want to be a writer," she announced slowly and softly, "*un*like Dad. But it's a secret," she added quickly, her voice rising, indicating importance.

Godbee tipped the brim of her straw hat back. "How wonderful," she whispered. "That's great. A writer."

Martha widened her eyes at the sea and blinked. Telling someone made it seem real. She nibbled on her bottom lip, holding back a smile.

"I didn't even bring books to read this year," said Martha. "So I can write."

"My," said Godbee, "that's serious. "Well. It's hard for me to think of you without your nose buried in a book. What book was it last year?"

"*To Kill a Mockingbird.* I've read it ten times, at least."

The book had been her father's when he was a teenager, his name inscribed on the inside front cover in a messy boyish scrawl. More than a few times, Martha had run her finger over his signature, pondering the impossibility that her father could ever have been her age, been anything but her father.

The sun was reflected in Godbee's bifocals for a second, causing them to go white, and when she turned her head slightly, Martha could see they were speckled with sand. "What do you want to write?" asked Godbee. "Or, I should say, what have you written?"

"Not much. Mostly school things, which

don't really count." Martha paused, searching for the right words. "I'd like to write novels."

"Why are you keeping it a secret?"

"Well, I didn't want Dad to think I was copying him. And now *that* doesn't matter. But I don't know— Maybe I'm waiting— I guess I'm waiting till I write something kind of long before I tell everyone. Something good."

"Any ideas?"

"Hmm," Martha breathed. Suddenly her mind was elsewhere. Her mind was working.

A wind started up, making Godbee's hat twitch and setting the rosebushes in the garden aflutter. It was relatively early, but already the roses were baking in the sun, and their smell, which carried on the wind, was intense and full, perfumey like maraschino cherries.

Martha was staring. Her vision was awash with red rose petals.

"Are you with me, sweetie?" asked Godbee.

"Oh, yeah," Martha replied, obviously distracted. "I was just thinking about my novel. It's about this girl named Olive."

18
Faraway

"There is, most definitely," said Godbee, "a faraway look in your eyes. I think you need to work on your book." Her forehead was set with wrinkles that formed an inverted chevron, the deeply etched point sitting directly above the bridge of her nose.

"Huh?"

Godbee nodded away from them, toward the water. "Go," she said. "Be a writer." She stood, and her dress billowed like a sail. She held on to her hat. "I'll go read or putter in the garden."

Less than ten minutes later, Martha was lying on her beach towel on a big flat rock by the sea, ready to write. It was only then that it dawned on her that she hadn't given Godbee the chance to share her bit of information, to do her telling for the day. "Later," Martha said to herself, "I'll ask her later." She opened her notebook and began.

The girl arrived alone at the ocean.

No. Martha turned to a clean page and started over.

The girl had run away. She ended up at the sea with only her backpack and

No. Martha sucked on her pen cap, made it whistle. She remembered that Olive's first sentence was about an orphan. Tried again.

Her name was Olive. She arrived at her grandmother's house in tears. She was an orphan. She held her grandmother's old wrinkly hands and wept. Then she heard the ocean. She looked up as a giant wave crashed on a giant rock, and for a moment she forgot how sad she was.

Martha could think of nothing else to write. She closed her notebook and her eyes and fell asleep in the hot, hot sun.

19
Jimmy Manning

Laughing and hooting and whistling and yelping.

Martha woke from a dream in which she had been walking underwater. When she opened her eyes and sat up, the moist, salty air surrounded her like a cocoon and pushed against her the way the water in her dream had, as if the dream was wearing off gradually and she would have to move in slow motion for a long minute.

More noises. Silly boy sounds. Martha heard her name and turned.

Her brother, Vince, and all five Manning brothers—Jimmy, Tate, Todd, Luke, and Leo—were running along the beach. Jimmy, the oldest, was leading, holding a video camera. The two youngest—Luke and Leo—were making the most noise. They jabbed at each other with open hands. They kicked. They grunted and shrieked. They yelled, "Karate! Chop! Chop!"

"Martha!" She couldn't tell who it was calling her.

Martha tossed her notebook and sunscreen into her backpack, knotted her towel around her waist, and headed in the direction of the boys, pulled by curiosity. She wanted to know what they were doing. She wanted to get a good look at Tate Manning.

When she got close enough to see the Mannings clearly and remember their faces, it wasn't Tate who interested her, but Jimmy. She gazed at him one beat too long. And he looked at her and looked away, smiling.

"What are you doing?" Martha asked, her eyes flitting from head to head.

"Jimmy's making a film," said Vince.

"We're in it," said Leo. He made a goofy face and took a bow.

"It's called *The World Is Not What You Think It Is,*" said Jimmy proudly. One eyebrow arched; one corner of his mouth turned upward.

When she heard his voice, she realized it was he who had called her name, and this thought made her mind go blank for a moment.

The next thing she knew Jimmy was looking at her with searching eyes, saying, "Well?"

What had she missed? She didn't know what he was referring to, but she could tell he was waiting for an answer. She echoed him, hoarsely, "Well?"

"Well?" he repeated. "Do you? Do you want to come over to my house and see part of my film?" In a whisper, he added, "We could ditch these guys."

Her tongue was pasted to the roof of her mouth, all the moisture having been drained out. She was afraid that if she tried to answer, all she could manage would be a dry cough. She nodded. And worked at a smile.

20

The World Is Not What You Think It Is

Mindlessly Martha formed a steeple out of her fingers, the way she had as a child doing hand rhymes. *This is the church, this is the steeple* . . . She touched her nose with the steeple, then dropped her hands to her lap.

She was absorbed by Jimmy's video, and equally absorbed by the fact that Jimmy Manning himself sat less than half a couch away from her, his chin thrust out, making him look important. She could smell his sunscreen (coconutty) and his chewing gum (grape). Without moving her head, she stole peeks at him. When he shifted, settling deeper into the couch, then leaning forward again, his dark blond hair flapped like fringe over his eyes. And she decided his green eyes were like broken glass.

Martha played with her hands some more, became aware of them, jammed them under her thighs, forgot them.

"The world is not what you think it is," a

voice repeated. Martha guessed it was Jimmy's voice, altered somehow, making him sound mechanical, roboticized. The images that flashed slowly across the screen were of water and sand and sun and dramatic clouds. Of gulls and driftwood and patchy beds of sea grass shivering in the wind. The most remarkable scenes, in Martha's opinion, were of wind-sculpted dunes, uniform and vast, lined up like buns in a bakery, and of white shafts of light, ladders leading from the ocean to the sky. Martha recognized some of the scenes—the cove, the harbor; there was even a glimpse of Godbee's roses above the seawall.

Then the tone of the images took a turn. The screen was crammed with people and parking lots and garbage. And the images changed from one to the next abruptly, quickly. An enormous man, rolls and rolls of him spilling out of his bathing suit, jiggling as he passed. A long-haired woman, bony, tanned dark brown, wearing a bikini and sunglasses and pulling a screaming toddler behind her. A girl, about ten years old, with tear-streaked cheeks and crossed arms, poking her toes at the water's foamy edge, saying, "I will not! I will not!" Throughout it all, Jimmy's voice: "Nature. Isn't it beautiful? Nature. Isn't it beautiful?"

The screen went black for a few seconds. "That was the nature part," Jimmy whispered. He cracked his knuckles, snapped his gum. "The family part comes next."

The family part began with a shot of the Mannings' dining room. Martha knew the room from the handful of times her family had shared a meal with the Mannings over the years. She knew the wallpaper—a stylized pattern of willow branches with mustard-colored birds hiding among the leaves. At one of these meals, Martha had been so bored she tried to count the birds, then imagined she was one of them, darting in and out of the labyrinthine foliage. Now she wondered how she could ever have been bored sitting at the same table as Jimmy Manning.

The camera zoomed in on a framed photograph hanging on the wall. It was a recent portrait of the Mannings, everyone smiling, looking eager. Jimmy's recorded voice was back, mingling with sugary music. "The world is not what you think it is. The world is not . . ."

Martha mouthed the words while a photograph of Mr. and Mrs. Manning, on their wedding day, came and went, followed by a separate, framed photograph of each of the five Manning boys as babies. Bald, round, dimpled. All ten eyes long-lashed and twinkling. Definitely brothers.

The music stopped.

Next came a live scene, a scene showing Jimmy's parents from a distance, through a doorway. Late sunlight fell across them, staining them and everything beyond the shadowed door frame golden. The camera moved closer. Mrs. Manning was crying, pounding her fist on a table. Mr. Manning faced her across the table, his hands flying about like crazed birds. Then he locked his fingers behind his neck and froze.

Mrs. Manning: "Well . . . say something. *Say* something!"

Mr. Manning:

Mrs. Manning: "Say *any*thing!"

Mr. Manning:

Mrs. Manning: "You always do this."

Suddenly Jimmy's parents sensed the camera, turned toward it. Jimmy's mother covered her face and walked away. His father approached, outraged. "Turn that damned thing off!" he yelled. "You little— Damn it!" He reached out and his hand grew—big and dark as a boxing glove—filling the screen.

Martha could tell the camera was being jerked around, fought over.

The voice-over: "Families. Aren't they wonderful?"

Then there were interviews with Tate, Todd, Luke, and Leo. Each interview was shot against a plain white background.

Tate: "I don't have anything to say. I hate video cameras." Pause. "You're a prick, Jimmy. How's that?"

Before Tate slipped out of view (eyes rolling), there was a blurry close-up of his blemished chin—sallow in this particular light—focusing on an enormous whitehead.

Todd: "Dad, the dictator, yells too much. More than anyone in the world. Except, that is, for Mom, the screamer, who wins that prize, hands down.

"I guess I'd like to be an orphan and live with a *very* rich family in a *huge* mansion. And not have to go to school. Yeah, that would be cool."

Luke and Leo were filmed together.

Luke: "Leo is always copying me."

Leo: "I do not."

Luke: "Yes, you do."

Leo: "No, I don't."

Luke: *"No, I don't."*

Leo: "Stop that!"

Luke: "Stop that!"

Leo: "See, *you're* the copier!"

Luke: "See, *you're* the copier!"

Leo: "Shut up!"

Luke: "Shut up!"

Leo: "I *hate* you!"

Luke: "I *hate* you!"

Push.

Push.

Hit.

Hit.

Leo: "Mom!"

Luke: "Mom!"

Empty white wall.

The voice-over again: "Families. Aren't they wonderful?"

21

Private Moments

"That's as far as I've gotten," Jimmy told Martha. He turned off the television and the VCR. He blew a translucent purplish blue bubble with his gum.

"It's really good," said Martha. "Your video." And she truly meant it. Maybe, she thought, it's even profound.

"I haven't shown it to my parents."

"Yeah," said Martha. She'd guessed as much. The scene with Mr. and Mrs. Manning had given her the chills, and yet she realized that any family, even the very best ones, had their moments. Awful, private moments. Had them every day. Many times a day. What if dinner at Godbee's the previous night had been captured on film? The thought embarrassed Martha to her very core. "Yeah," she repeated. She couldn't think of anything better to say. Why was coming up with a simple sentence so difficult sometimes?

"I have to finish the family part," said

Jimmy, "fine-tune it. And then I'll work on the death part," he explained. "And the love part." He grinned at her. An inscrutable grin.

All Martha could think of was the word love. She heard it like an echo in her head, in Jimmy's voice. "I've got to go," said Martha rising. "I didn't tell my grandma where I was. She might be worrying."

"I'll call you," said Jimmy.

In an instant, Martha was out of the dark basement and into the bright light of day.

Suddenly Tate was right beside her. Had he followed her up the stairs? Had he been watching the video, too? He seemed to be on the verge of speaking. Finally he did. "I'm glad you came back," he said. "To your grandma's, I mean."

"Me, too."

In the silence that came next, the towel that had been knotted around Martha's waist fell to the ground, a pink mound at her ankles. She quickly repositioned the towel and retied the ends. Tight.

Tate looked around as if he had misplaced something. "Your, um, your towel is the same color as the lining of a shell," he said.

Martha nodded. "I guess . . . yes, it is," she said. She glanced back at the Mannings' house, scanning the windows, checking for Jimmy, then started to move on.

"Well, bye," said Tate, squinting, half waving, half saluting.

"Bye."

As Martha walked back to Godbee's, she said the word aloud: "Jimmy. Jimmy, Jimmy, Jimmy . . ." She said it until the tips of her ears were on fire and her heart expanded. She said it until it was just a sound with no meaning.

22
Taste and Smell

Because Jimmy Manning was on her mind, Martha forgot about her agreement with her grandmother until later in the day when Godbee passed Martha in the living room and said, "I can't taste anymore. Or smell."

Martha followed her grandmother through the room and down the narrow hallway. "But you put salt on your soup at dinner last night."

Godbee turned and smiled, the kindest smile, holding Martha with her eyes. "Out of habit, I suppose. Or wishful thinking." She waited. "Pretending."

Lucy, naked, ran by, flailing her arms and screeching. Martha's mother was right behind her, carrying a diaper. "Tornado at large," she said, twisting to get through.

At the same time, the telephone rang. Martha knew it was Jimmy.

"It's for you, Mom!" called Martha's father.

"Chaos," said Godbee, her shoulders lifting slightly. With a flourish, she raised her hand to

brush a strand of hair from her face. In a con-
tinuation of the elegant gesture, she tucked
the hair back into the silvery roll atop her head
and went to answer the phone.

And Martha was left to herself, imagining
for a moment that her grandmother was fad-
ing away. Disappearing.

23
Writing and Waiting

That night, while she waited for the phone to ring, Martha reread what she had written earlier.

Her name was Olive. She arrived at her grandmother's house in tears. She was an orphan. She held her grandmother's old wrinkly hands and wept. Then she heard the ocean. She looked up as a giant wave crashed on a giant rock and for a moment she forgot how sad she was.

And then she added the following:

But of course the sadness returned. And it stayed and stayed.

The grandmother was old and frail. Her fingers were like ginger roots. Olive tried to cook fabulous meals for her grandmother. Turkey dinners like Thanksgiving dinners. And baked ham with brown sugar like

Easter and Christmas.

"It's no use, darling," said the grandmother. "I can't taste anymore."

Olive tried to surprise her grandmother by filling her house with roses.

"Doesn't it smell beautiful?" said Olive.

"It's no use, darling," said the grandmother. "I can't smell anymore either."

Martha closed her notebook. She checked the telephone to make sure it was working properly. The dial tone hummed as it should. She went back to her notebook. She turned to the last page and wrote *Jimmy Jimmy Jimmy* until the page was completely filled, the long descenders of the ys linking one row of writing to the next as if they were stitched together.

And the telephone still didn't ring.

24
Fog

When Martha woke up, fog was drifting in off the ocean in clumps, misty islands coming ashore. She stood by the open window in the yellow room, hugging herself. Goose bumps cropped up all over her arms and legs.

The fog would burn off, the temperature would rise, and soon it would be a perfect August day, but as Martha watched the fog, she shivered and wondered about more important things.

Will I see Jimmy today?

What will I tell Godbee about me?

What will Godbee tell me?

25
Bottle

"Can I go now?" asked Vince, his mouth still full of food.

Martha stopped chewing and looked up.

"I don't know, *can* you?" said Martha's mother. She paused, smiled ironically. "Yes, you *may*."

"Whatever," Vince mumbled before bounding off.

"So much for enforced togetherness," said Martha's father.

"Never works," said Godbee. "Never did, as I recall."

Martha thought it had worked, at least in part. Even if Vince had been with them under duress, it had felt, in flashes, like old times. They had all gone swimming (except, of course, Godbee, who watched from her chair beneath her big umbrella on the shore), and afterward, together on the beach, had had a picnic lunch—two hampers and a cooler stuffed with odds and ends. Between swimming and eating, Martha had even tried to teach Lucy how to build houses on the rocks out of beach towels, blankets, and driftwood.

"Vince and I used to do this every day," Martha told her sister. "Every day that we were here visiting Godbee. Since forever."

Without being prompted, Vince had run to catch up with his sisters. "I'll help!" he had shouted. And he did. For about ten minutes. "You really have to wedge the wood in place. Make it secure. When the wind blows, the towels look like sails."

"Or a whole city of wrecked ships," said Martha. "That's what I used to think."

Then, as if the wind had shifted or the temperature had suddenly dropped, Vince said, "There, I've fulfilled my duty. Bye, girls!" and strolled back to their parents and Godbee, who were laying out the food on an old quilt.

Without Vince, Martha had lost her enthusiasm for the project, and during lunch she watched the half-completed encampment tilt slowly and collapse.

"Kaboom," said Vince.

Martha pretended not to care.

Then Vince was gone. Literally.

And then Lucy was gone. She'd fallen asleep on the picnic blanket, curled into a fist at Martha's side.

And then Martha's parents were gone, too. They decided to take advantage of Lucy's nap and go for a short walk. They headed up the beach holding hands, arms swinging, stepping in and out of breaking waves.

"Just us women again," said Godbee.

Martha smiled.

"Nice."

Martha plucked the last orange segment from the plastic container near her foot and popped it into her mouth. She tried not to taste the orange, breathing through her nose instead of her mouth, as if this would somehow shut off her sense of taste. The wings of her nostrils flared—a sign of her deep concentration. She coughed as she swallowed, and nearly choked. She couldn't do it; she couldn't not taste the orange. She sniffed her fingers— orange. Orange laced the air.

"Do you remember what an orange tastes like?" Martha asked.

"Hmm."

Martha waited uncertainly. Maybe she

shouldn't have asked the question.

Finally Godbee nodded. "Yes," she replied, "yes. I can't smell the ocean or run along the beach anymore either, but I remember what those things were like, too. Strange, I remember certain feelings and sensations more clearly the further away from them I become." She shrugged politely. "How's your writing?"

"It's hard," said Martha. "But I've got a start."

"Starting is the most difficult part," said Godbee. "Good. Are you willing to share it?"

Martha hesitated, canting her head to one side. Would Godbee be offended by the grandmother with ginger-root fingers in her story?

"I'll wait until you're ready," Godbee said. "You know, I wanted to be a writer at one point in my life, too. It must run through the Boyle blood."

"You did?"

"I even wrote a short story. Just one. It was about a girl who moved with her family, away from the ocean to a new home far inland. The girl was despondent about having to leave her beloved ocean, so she filled a bottle with seawater and carried it with her when she moved.

She kept the bottle on her bedside table in the new house."

Godbee stopped and frowned. She sighed. "I couldn't figure out how to end it," she continued, her voice slightly wheezy, "so I had her accidentally knock the bottle off the table, to shatter across the floor."

"And then what happened?"

"That's it."

"That's it?"

"Not very good, I agree."

"No. I think it's *great*." Martha was even a bit jealous. She thought Godbee's story was far better than hers. Although Martha would have had the mother be the one to break the bottle. Maybe even on purpose.

Lucy whimpered and twitched like a puppy.

"You know," Godbee whispered, nodding toward Lucy, "I ate a jar of your sister's bananas early this morning while the house was still asleep. Just for kicks."

Martha laughed.

"Oh dear," said Godbee. "Now, I've gone and told you *two* things about me, and I've yet to hear anything new from someone I know and love. . . ." She looked at Martha steadily.

There was affection and amusement in her eyes.

For some reason Martha lost all control; she couldn't stop the words from pouring from her mouth: "I think I like Jimmy Manning."

26
Lucky

The moment of the telling passed, and Martha was still alive: She hadn't burst into flames; the earth hadn't opened up beneath her feet and swallowed her whole. And Godbee hadn't laughed or sighed or clutched her heart sarcastically.

"Lucky him," was what Godbee said evenly. "Lucky him."

27
Kyle Gilbert

Only one other time, since she was old enough for it to matter, had Martha told someone she liked a boy. The other time, the other telling, had led to complete embarrassment. The actual telling hadn't been the problem; the problem came later.

Kyle Gilbert was his name. And the only person Martha had told was Holly.

"He's okay," Holly had said, unfazed by the confession. "But he's got two first names. Weird."

"Only you would think of that," said Martha. But it didn't ruin anything for her. And she was glad to have confided in Holly. It made her feelings more real somehow.

Martha kept the information from everyone else but sometimes felt that her thoughts concerning Kyle Gilbert were emblazoned on her forehead or visible above her head in a cartoon cloud.

"Have you told him yet?" Holly asked. And

asked again. "Kyle—or is it Gilbert?"

In response, Martha would roll her eyes or toss her head or make the most awful face possible.

"I could tell him," Holly offered. "Or we could get someone to pass it on."

"NO," was Martha's emphatic reply.

Then, on a Friday in April (the fourteenth, to be exact, as if she'd ever forget), as Martha and Holly waited by their lockers before classes began, organizing their books for first period, Holly said, "Martha, um, Kyle Gilbert is here."

Martha was stooped, hunched forward, her head halfway inside the dark locker. "Yeah, right," she replied. There was the slightest echo.

"I'm ser-i-ous," Holly said. Her voice was soft but high.

Martha made kissing sounds. "I love you, Kyle," she said jokingly as she stood and whirled around. She found herself face to face with Kyle Gilbert.

Martha's stomach rippled. "Oh—my—God," she said, but wasn't sure if anyone heard her. The words were lost in a tunnel inside her. Blood flooded to her neck and face. A burning sensation started in her chest and moved upward. Her hands were white and clammy.

"Sorry," said Kyle Gilbert, "I just wanted to ask you a question about the assignment for Messina's class." His expression was blank, like that of a dog, then his eyes bounced around without settling anywhere for more than a couple seconds. "Catch you later," he said, shaking his head. "Much," he added, walking quickly down the hall. Two of his friends were with him, laughing and digging their fingers into his sides. "Oooh, oooh," one of them said, the voice dripping with fake sweetness. "I love you, Kyle."

I wish I were dead, thought Martha.

She thought it all morning, all afternoon. She couldn't concentrate on her schoolwork. She was convinced that everyone at Susan B. Anthony Middle School knew what had happened. Everything—laughter in the cafeteria, whispering in the rest rooms, a shove in the hallway—confirmed her suspicion. She thought she might cry. Or run out the front doors and keep running.

"Who cares?" said Holly.

"Like you wouldn't?" said Martha.

"Just trying to help."

Things got worse in communication arts class. With only five minutes to go before school would be over, Ms. Driggs announced the homework assignment for the weekend. "Listen, everyone," she said, her voice straining over the chatter and buzzing. "In your journals, I'd like you to write about your most embarrassing moment. Be descriptive. Make me feel as if I were there with you."

Moans and groans erupted throughout the classroom. Some laughter, too.

"How long does it have to be?" asked Moira Shanstine.

Martha couldn't believe it. A new wave of doom rushed over her. Her heartbeat quickened, like a bird's. She hated Ms. Driggs, someone she usually liked. Driggs, dregs, rotten eggs. Dead.

Furtively Martha surveyed the room. People were whispering, snickering. Everyone knew about her. For some reason her eyes connected with Olive Barstow's and locked. The look on Olive's face was one of complete horror. Even Olive Barstow knew. Even she was overcome with Martha's shame and shock. Seconds passed before Martha looked elsewhere. Her composure was wearing thin. She felt desperate.

And then, with the suddenness of a sneeze, Martha did something uncharacteristic. She was thinking out loud, being reckless. Without raising her hand, she stood and said, "But it's not fair. It's just not fair, Ms. Driggs." Her heart pounded in her throat. "Why should we bare our souls and share our secrets for your entertainment? It's just—wrong." Tears welled in her eyes. Her voice wavered. "Really." She collapsed in her desk.

Ms. Driggs looked at Martha over her glasses. She wrinkled her nose the way Lucy would. "You have a point," she said. She took a deep breath, then exhaled upward, blowing at her bangs. She smiled brightly at Martha with her crisp pink lips. "Okay, okay. Let's see— how about a character sketch. Listen, every-one, write a character sketch of someone over fifty or under five. Someone you know well. Make him or her come alive for me."

All at once the bell rang and people cheered

and Moira Shanstine asked, "How long does it have to be?" and someone said, "Martha Boyle for president."

Martha was a wreck, but she felt triumphant, too.

On the way home, Holly said, "You could've just written about something else, you know. Made something up."

"I know."

"But anyway," said Holly, "you were good. You were really good."

28
Initials

Godbee didn't mention Jimmy Manning again, which was exactly as Martha wished it to be.

After the remnants of the picnic had been gathered and brought home, the day passed quietly and slowly. Martha looked for shells and found some of her favorites—lady slippers and thin, pearly jingle shells. She wrote Kyle Gilbert's initials with a stick in the wet, shiny sand within the ocean's reach. It only took the sweeping of three waves for the initials to be washed away. She wrote Jimmy Manning's initials up beyond the tideline. Safe. She went to the general store with her father and Lucy to get ice-cream sandwiches. She walked to the marsh and the small stone jetty and the outcropping of rock that always reminded her of burly animals huddled together in sleep. And she sat on Godbee's window seat doing nothing at all, the expression in her eyes remote, her thoughts drifting mindlessly.

When the telephone rang, her thoughts were still elsewhere, and when she heard Vince's voice on the other end, she was instantly disappointed.

"Oh, hi," she said flatly.

"Will you ask Mom if I can stay at the Mannings' again?" said Vince. "For dinner and overnight. We're having lobsters and clams, and then we're camping out."

"*You* ask her," said Martha, her heart sinking for many reasons.

"Is she there?"

"Somewhere," replied Martha. "Hang on." She walked up the back hallway, stretching the telephone cord to its limit. She didn't see or hear anyone.

"Are you still there?" Vince asked impatiently.

"I'm looking, I'm looking," said Martha. Her face tightened. She was about to add, "*You* come and find her. I'm not your slave," when Vince cut in.

"Oh," he said, "I almost forgot. You're invited for dinner, too. Jimmy said to ask you."

Martha's face cleared. Just like that.

She quickly found her mother and was

granted permission. She told Vince. Then, in a flurry, she checked herself in the mirror, grabbed her sweater so that she would have something to hold on to, yelled good-bye, and was out the door and on her way.

29
Lobster

A royal bout of shyness hit Martha as she stepped onto the Mannings' porch and heard voices from within the house. Before she had the chance to ring the bell or knock, Tate opened the door, and it occurred to Martha that he'd been stationed there, waiting.

"Hi," he said.

"Hi." She had been inside these very walls just yesterday, and yet it felt as though she were entering new territory.

Tate let Martha pass in front of him, then, seconds later, awkwardly scrambled past her and led her to the kitchen.

The room was bright and noisy. People stood in clusters by the table, sink, and stove. There were several children and adults Martha didn't know. Mrs. Manning yelled hello above the racket, and Mr. Manning patted her head, the way she thought he might greet a five-year-old, or Lucy. Jimmy nodded at Martha over his shoulder, then motioned for her to join him. "I'm filming death," he said. "You made it just in time."

Martha came up behind Jimmy. From across the room it had appeared as if smoke were rising from his head. Martha craned her neck and lifted herself up on her toes. Now she could see—steam roiled upward from a huge pot on the stove, and Mrs. Manning's hand was poised above it, clutching a lobster.

"Capital punishment for crustaceans," said Jimmy, aiming his camera, zooming in.

"Oh, hush," said his mother. "Really."

On contact with the water, the lobster convulsed.

"Ooh," said a woman, turning away, her face pinched. "That always gives me the creeps. Makes me think of epileptic seizures."

Martha had watched lobsters cook many times before, usually at Godbee's, and had been oddly fascinated by it, and sometimes ashamed, too. Mrs. Maxwell, the woman who cleaned house for Godbee weekly and checked on her daily when Martha's family wasn't visiting, had once taught Martha how to paralyze a lobster before steaming it, by standing it upside down on its head and rubbing its back.

"It's crude anesthesia," Mrs. Maxwell had said, "but it works."

"I need a better aerial shot," said Jimmy. He pulled a chair over to the stove and climbed up, towering over the pot.

"Let me see," said Leo. "Let me see."

"Death," said Jimmy. "Red death."

"I don't think their brains are very big," said Mrs. Manning, her voice taking on an angry tone. She bumped Jimmy's chair slightly, more for effect than anything else.

"Hey," said Jimmy. "Careful."

"Come on, move. I've got a lot of these to do."

"Murder at the Mannings'," said Jimmy. "A massacre."

"The only murder of consequence will be yours," said Mrs. Manning. She sighed dramatically. "Okay. Enough. Out of the kitchen. I mean it. Out. Before I take that camera and plunge it into the pot."

Jimmy clicked the camera off. "Perfect, Mom," he said. "Thank you. I couldn't have staged it better myself."

30
Blue

Blue. It seemed to Martha that everything was blue. The sea. The sky, turning. The sand and grass and leaves. The air. Even the sounds. Blue.

"You're in space," said Jimmy.

Martha turned. "Huh?"

"You . . . are . . . in . . . space. Gone. Out there."

"Oh, I was just thinking that—" She stopped herself from saying "everything is blue." He'd think she was an idiot. "—that I'm full," she finally said.

"Me, too."

"So, you're not really against killing lobsters, right? I mean, you ate a lot."

Jimmy shrugged and fought back a grin. "I guess." When he moved his head a certain way, a spot on his chin shone. Melted butter.

"You *love* lobsters," said Tate. "You're such a faker."

"Get lost," said Jimmy.

"You." Tate's eyes were indignant.

"I mean it," said Jimmy.

And so Tate mumbled something to Vince, then collected his dirty plate and utensils and walked off, back toward the house, followed by Vince, Todd, Luke, Leo, and some Manning cousins. Which left Martha and Jimmy alone, sitting on one of the long benches near the edge of the yard, just above the beach, at the hem of tall grass and dogged weeds.

The adults were eating separately from the children, inside the house. The sound of their laughter rose and fell like waves.

"Let's go," said Jimmy. "We could walk to the Benton place."

"What about our dishes?" asked Martha.

"Oh, just leave them. Someone'll pick them up. Or we can get them later." Jimmy grabbed his video camera. "Come on."

31

The Benton Place

The Benton property was inland, about halfway between the Mannings' and Godbee's. To get to it, you had to walk along the shore, then cut in through a marshy area (by way of a boardwalk), climb over a stone wall, cross a field of dingy grass, go around the far-reaching limbs of a huge beech tree, take a short path of crushed shells, and squeeze through a creaky iron gate.

In the field, Martha played a game. She sped up; so did Jimmy. She slowed down; he did, too. He matched her, stride for stride. At one point, when she quickened her pace, he tugged on her sleeve. She became aware of the pump of her heart.

"The death section of my film is pretty weak, I admit," Jimmy told her. He swatted at something in the air as he talked. They were rounding the beech tree. "I've got some shots of a dead gull baking in the sun, and lots of dead fish. Fish guts, too. And now the lobster.

But what I really need is a person."

"A person? A real, dead person?"

He waited a long time before he answered. Broken shells crunched under their feet. "No. Of course not."

"Oh." Thank God, she thought. "Right."

"Maybe someone about to die, or something. I don't know. Someone old."

Jimmy turned sidewise and passed through the narrow gap between the gate and its post, holding his camera high. A rusty, padlocked loop of chain, on the ground, connected the gate to the post and kept the gate from opening wide. "Maybe I could interview your grandma."

Martha's shirt had caught on a metal curlicue as she followed Jimmy through the gate. "No," she said firmly. She pulled her shirt, heard it rip, freed it. "What about *your* grandparents?"

"Too young."

Martha examined her shirt. There was a hole the size of a paper clip. "Godbee wouldn't want to be interviewed about dying. And she's so healthy, she'll probably outlive both of us."

Jimmy looked as though he were going to

say something else, but instead gave a little *humph* and walked ahead.

They had arrived.

The Benton house was simple and boxy, sided with cedar shakes that had weathered to a soft gray. Patches of new shakes—brown—cropped up here and there like bandages, giving the house a sad, wounded look. Several ramshackle outbuildings surrounded the house, including a low-roofed, open-sided, L-shaped structure that was segmented into stalls. Firewood and rotting tables filled it.

Martha had always known this building as "the stable" and when she was little, she'd pretended it was home to a herd of ponies made of clear glass, barely visible, and only to her. Godbee had said it had been the site of a flea market long ago.

The current owners lived in Chicago and rarely came to visit. Martha had never seen them.

Darkness was setting in. Security lights hanging from poles clicked on and hummed like electric moons. Martha and Jimmy stood near a pollarded apple tree that cast a strange shadow and made Martha think of a person with his head chopped off.

"It's kind of spooky here," said Martha. "At this time of day."

"Definitely haunted," said Jimmy. "A good place to film something about death—*if* there was something to film." He paused only a second, then asked, "Hey, what do you think happens after you die?"

The question surprised Martha. "I don't know," she said. She felt completely ignorant, all of a sudden, of all things that mattered. "I wish—" she said with some effort. "I wish people didn't have to die."

And at that moment thoughts of Olive came to her in a rush.

And before she knew it, Martha was leaning against the stable, within a cone of light, talking about Olive Barstow.

And Jimmy was filming her.

32

Recording

Jimmy framed Martha, zoomed in until her face filled the viewfinder. "Louder," he said. "Talk louder."

Martha had started with Olive's mother's visit and told everything she knew—the words running steadily out of her mouth as though her mouth were a faucet and someone had turned it on—jumping around from the journal page and its coincidences to what she knew of the accident to Olive's mother's old bicycle to how Olive had been mistreated or ignored at school.

She said: "Now I wish I had known her better."

She said: "I'll never know why she thought I was so nice."

She said: "My friend Holly thinks she was weird, but I think she was just different from everyone else. Not in a bad way."

She said: "I'll keep the journal page forever."

She said: "Twelve is too young to die."

The words were stopping, and she was left with a hollow space inside her. She felt boneless. Tears pricked her eyes, and she blinked rapidly. She sidestepped out of the direct light. As darkness tightened around her, the knowledge she had buried became vividly realized: If Olive could die, then so could I. So could anybody. Anytime.

"I don't want to die," she said, and turned away from the camera.

33
Holding Hands

"That was great," said Jimmy, smiling. He couldn't hide his glee. He raised his fist above his head in a triumphant gesture. "Yes."

"I want to go home," said Martha.

They barely spoke the entire way. And Martha barely noticed the ceiling of stars or the sound of the surf. She was aware, however, of the cool wind that had started up. She shivered. She realized that she didn't have her sweater. She remembered it being draped over her shoulders when they first arrived at the Benton place. I must have lost it by the stable, she thought. She liked her sweater but had no inclination to go back and look for it now. She'd get it tomorrow. She just wanted to be with other people. People she loved. Happy people. Lots of people.

Earlier she had thought everything was blue, and now she thought everything was black, as if she had been dropped into a dark hole. The world was cold and harsh and unpredictable. She shivered again.

"Tomorrow I'm filming at the Benton place again," said Jimmy, breaking the silence. "I'm starting the love section, and you're helping me. I need you." Then he took her hand and held it.

A current of excitement, and one of self-consciousness, ran through Martha. There was a strange sensation in her belly, too.

The night had taken another turn.

Jimmy's grip was loose. So loose that Martha wondered if her hand would slip away from his. She wondered if she should squeeze his hand but decided that that would be too bold.

Something kept her from actually looking at her hand, although she was tempted to. She aimed her gaze straight ahead. But she thought about her hand until it became separate from her, a small, limp creature unto itself.

He didn't let go.

The marshy area ended. When they got to the beach, Jimmy led Martha in the direction of his house, not Godbee's, but Martha didn't mind. If Jimmy Manning kept holding her hand, she could have walked all the way to Provincetown.

His hand was warm.

They came upon a group of adults circling a bonfire. The flames lit the ring of faces, turning the faces orange. There was one child among the adults—a little girl, marching in place, holding a sparkler in each hand. The girl made eye contact with Martha and smiled shyly. Martha smiled back, feeling very grown-up.

He started swinging his arm, drawing Martha's into the rhythm.

As they passed the group, Martha heard one of the men say, "Ah, embryonic love." The man chuckled and nodded at Martha and Jimmy. Another man laughed softly.

Martha wasn't completely certain what the comment meant, but she knew the man was being condescending, in the very way adults so often are.

"Jerks," said Jimmy under his breath. The arm swinging stopped. "Ancient moronic jerk-offs," he added, tightening his grip on Martha's hand and walking faster. "They're probably all over forty."

"And who ever heard of bionic doves, anyway," Martha joked in a hollow, mature-sounding voice. The second the words were spoken, she regretted having said them. She had tried to be funny, clever, but knew she had failed miserably. If embarrassment were a noise, sirens would be blaring from every one of my pores, she thought.

To Martha's relief, Jimmy didn't seem to notice. "I should film *them*," he said, "and call it *The World Is Full of Assholes.*"

"Yeah."

"I'm going to be a famous filmmaker someday. Like Stanley Kubrick. Have you seen his film *2001: A Space Odyssey*? I've seen it about twenty-eight times."

"I think I saw parts of it on TV," said Martha.

"Well, you should see the whole thing. It's a masterpiece. I've got a tape. You could—"

Abruptly Martha pulled her hand away. In the near distance, she saw her father standing at the border of the Mannings' lawn. "My dad," she said.

"Hi!" her father called, walking toward them.

Quickly and quietly, Jimmy acknowledged Martha's father, and stepped aside. "So don't forget—tomorrow we're filming again." And then he raced off toward the lights of his house.

"What's up?" asked Martha's father. He smiled, raising his eyebrows, as if he knew the answer.

"Nothing."

"I didn't mean to interfere or surprise you," he said. He tilted his head, sending a sympathetic glance. "I'd come to the Mannings' to walk you home. We hadn't made a plan; you left the house so quickly."

Martha wiggled her fingers, and then—she couldn't help herself—she raised her fingers to her nose and sniffed them. To hide the intent of the gesture, she scratched the tip of her nose.

"You look cold. Want my jacket?"

"No, that's okay."

"Are you sure?"

She nodded.

For what seemed like a long time, they simply stood, facing the endless black ocean. After a deafeningly quiet moment (despite the roar of the waves), Martha said, "I'm tired," because she thought she should say something. And her statement was true—her eyelids were as heavy as stones, her shoulders were sagging.

"You look it."

"Let's go home."

"Good idea," said her father. They started off. "You know," he said, "when you were little and tired like this, I'd throw you over my shoulder and carry you home like a sack of rice. Sometimes I wish you were still that little. I wish I could still do that."

"Da-ad. That is so embarrassing," is what she said. But sometimes she wished it, too. Sometimes she wished it with all her heart.

34
Impossible

Martha was exhausted, and yet she had a difficult time falling asleep. Over and over she saw the movie of herself walking hand in hand with Jimmy Manning on the beach, a continuous loop playing in her head. Believing it was impossible.

She woke many times throughout the night—her arms prickly and at odd angles, the sheet twisted tightly around her ankles, the pillow on the floor—and only fell into a deep sleep as the sun began to rise.

35

Sparkler

The light in the room was very bright, too bright—she knew that the instant she opened her eyes. It was already late morning, she guessed, but she stayed in bed awhile longer, writing in her notebook, continuing Olive's story.

Olive's life changed forever the day she met the mysterious James. They met on the beach at a picnic that Olive's grandmother organized. Her grandmother wanted Olive to meet new people, so Olive could forget she was an orphan and finally start living a happy life.

There was the most food Olive had ever seen. James refused to eat the lobsters, saying he couldn't eat a formerly living creature. He stuck to fruits and vegetables.

After the picnic, as night came upon them, James built a huge bonfire. All the guests danced in a circle around the fire, holding sparklers.

The sparklers were as white as diamonds. They were like white hot chrysanthemums dripping onto the sand.

The sparklers were done. The fire was burning out. Most of the guests had left. And then James grabbed Olive's hand. And he held it for an hour. They walked up and down the beach. Olive's hand felt afire, like she was holding a sparkler against her skin.

36
Asking and Telling

"Where is everyone?" asked Martha.

"Good morning to you, too, sweetheart," said her mother.

"Morning, Mom," said Martha. "So where is everyone?"

"Dad and Godbee took their annual trip to the cemetery to check the plantings on Grandpa's grave. Lucy went with them. Vince went sailing."

"With who?"

"Brian Manning and some of the boys."

"Oh," said Martha, feeling the familiar blossoming of disappointment in the center of her belly. Why didn't Mr. Manning ask her? And what about Jimmy?

"But not *all* the boys," said her mother. "Jimmy called for you."

"He did? Why didn't you tell me? Why didn't you wake me up?" Martha played with her hair, because if she didn't, her fingers might break something.

"I invited him for lunch. He'll be here at noon."

"You *did*?" Martha couldn't decide if this pleased her or not.

"I did. Tell me what you'd like to eat."

"I'll think about it."

A pause.

Martha's mother ran her finger round and round the rim of her mug. "Is Jimmy Manning nice?"

Martha blushed. "Yes!" she said defensively. She crossed the room and stood in profile by the window.

"Just a simple question," said her mother. "This isn't an inquisition." She blew a kiss to her daughter from across the kitchen table. "I was just asking," she said, her voice as light as could be.

"I was just telling," said Martha.

37

Free

Martha was glad that her father, Lucy, and Godbee returned from the cemetery in time for lunch. Especially Godbee. Before that, while setting the table, Martha's mother had asked Jimmy question after question, as if she were interviewing him for her radio program. Martha listened, clicking her teeth, desperate to shrink to the size of a fly or for her mother to suddenly be struck dumb.

"How are your parents?"

"Okay, I guess."

"Are you looking forward to school starting?"

"Not really."

"How old are you now?"

"Fourteen."

"What *is* that near your elbow?"

"This? A Magic Marker film reel. It's going to be the logo for my production company. When I perfect it, I want to get a permanent tattoo."

With Godbee there, things changed. She didn't ask stupid questions. And she was the one to end the awkward silences; she made them all laugh with her sharp opinions (which seemed mostly an act to Martha) and her funny stories.

Lucy was oddly shy. She spoke just once during lunch, declaring in a loud whisper: "Girls pretty; boys rusty."

Between bites, Martha watched her grandmother. In the noonday light, Godbee's neck and cheeks were netted with deep wrinkles, as if someone had stitched her up and pulled the thread taut. Despite the wrinkles, her face seemed completely untroubled.

And it was Godbee who mercifully ended lunch for Martha and Jimmy at the earliest possible moment. "Oh, why don't you two go and have fun," she said. "You've been polite and placating long enough. Go, go."

They were released. They flew out of the house. They were free.

38
The Best Day

They ran and ran and ran and ran until they could run no longer and collapsed on the beach, two laughing, gasping heaps. Martha's eyes were watery, from laughing so hard and because the temperature had dropped. It was a clear, crisp, cool afternoon.

"My sides are killing me," said Jimmy.

Martha tried to catch her breath. She couldn't speak yet. They lay on their backs, heads on arms, his right elbow and her left nearly touching. Martha gazed into the sky until the sky became the ocean and Martha, all turned around, hung above it, calmly, mysteriously aloft as if tethered by invisible rope.

"Do *you* think boys are rusty?" asked Jimmy.

Martha sat up, regaining her sense of place. She considered Jimmy's question. "Sometimes," she said. "Which also means sometimes not," she added.

"I can tell your dad's a lawyer," said Jimmy.

Inconspicuously at first, Martha dug in the

sand with just a couple fingers. Then she pinched together a ragged wall, encircling the small hole she had hollowed out. Next she started a tower, making wide arcs with her arms to gather the sand and using both hands as scoops.

"Castle?" asked Jimmy. There was a groove of skepticism near his mouth.

"Want to help?"

His eyes were like insects, flitting all around. He didn't answer, but he got on his hands and knees and joined in.

"Just so you know," said Jimmy, "no self-respecting fourteen-year-old would be caught dead making a sand castle without a little kid with them."

"Do you want me to get my sister?"

"No, no, that's not what I'm saying. I'm just saying I'm doing this for you."

"Don't do it for me."

"Okay, for *us.*"

Martha smiled, a bit sheepishly. The funny thing was, Martha did like sand castles. Not just the idea of them, but the actual building of them as well. Was it weird? she wondered. Was she too old for this? She also liked making paper chains and collecting snow globes. Perhaps most childish, she enjoyed arranging her many small containers of lip gloss, by color, on her bed, or organizing them into families. She'd pair the right colors and fragrances to form perfect unions. Then there'd be births. This was Martha's favorite part of the game—deciding who was born to whom. Then the children would marry, and it would all begin again until it looked as if Martha were diagramming an elaborate military maneuver on her bedspread. She'd taught the game to Lucy, legitimizing it, making it a nice, kind thing for a big sister to do with her baby sister. But she vowed then and there—on the beach with Jimmy Manning—to give it up. She'd never do it again. She was too old for that now. Definitely. But sand castles were a different story.

The castle rose and widened, an empire at the edge of the sea. When Martha said, "We need accessories," they hunted down good things, but nothing unusual: steamer clam shells, stones in various shades of beige and gray, brown seaweed, part of a crab shell, and enough sodden, splintered pieces of driftwood to crown the towers and build an imposing gate at the castle's front entrance.

Martha's fingers were breaded with sand and smelled brackish, from the seaweed. She clapped her hands and rubbed them together to clean them off, a scowl of concentration clouding her face. Holding hands with Jimmy seemed to have taken place a million years ago. If it had happened at all. She took a breath as if to speak, but no words came out.

"What?" said Jimmy.

"What? What?"

"You looked like you were going to say something."

"Where's your camera?" Martha asked. She'd noticed he didn't have it with him. "I thought we were filming today. I thought I was helping you."

"Are you ready? Okay, then, let's go. I didn't want to rush, but if you're ready, I'm ready."

They stood. "Hey," said Jimmy, nodding. "Let's crash it."

"Really? Our beautiful castle?"

"If we don't someone else will. Some stranger. *That* would be tragic. *We* built it. It's our responsibility."

Jimmy did most of the crashing. Martha held back, half-heartedly toppling a tower, feeling as though it wasn't just the castle that was going down. But then, as the night before, Jimmy grabbed her hand, and castle or not, Martha knew the day would be the best of her life. She even mouthed the words, silently: *This is the best day of my life.*

39

A Question

Jimmy wouldn't stop talking. His speaking engine had been idling, and now was revving up. Martha's worry about uncomfortable silences had drifted out of her mind.

They weren't holding hands any longer. They had picked up the camera at Jimmy's house, and a tripod, too. He needed both hands to carry his equipment. Martha thought to offer to carry the tripod—then they would each still have a free hand for holding—but she couldn't summon the courage to make the suggestion, afraid her motive would be obvious.

"I was thinking we'd go to the Benton place again," Jimmy had said.

"Oh, good," Martha had replied. "I left my sweater there last night. I hope I find it."

As they traveled the familiar route, Jimmy talked about things as disparate as the lack of interesting girls at his school ("none whatsoever") to the drunk man wandering through the bleachers at a Sox game at Fenway Park he'd been to earlier that summer. ("He was totally, completely, amazingly trashed, and he had a gargantuan pink nose with giant pores and veiny blue lines all over it.")

He told her that his mother never fished, hated it in fact, because when she was a girl, she had accidentally snagged the eyelid of the family dog with her hook as she practiced casting. ("Posy yelped and yelped and my mom says she still can hear yelping whenever she sees a fishing rod.")

He told her that when he was little, he had snipped their cat's whiskers off with scissors and announced to his parents that he had seen the cat suck in her whiskers with one big inward breath. ("*Schrrrp.* Just like that. They didn't believe me, of course.")

He told her that he couldn't wait to make it as a real director—and that he might even skip college—because he was so tired of having no money to speak of. ("My bank account totally sucks. I've got a trust fund from one of my grandpas, but I won't get that until I'm eighteen or twenty-one, or something.")

Jimmy covered it all: his favorite band, his

favorite classic rock band, his favorite songs of the decade and the century, his favorite TV shows, his favorite Web sites. He talked about the history and future of film and the difference between "films" and "movies."

Jimmy talked and Martha listened. And then Jimmy switched gears and asked Martha what she thought about many things, anything that came to his mind, and his voice was serious, as if her opinion were the most important thing and he really wanted to know.

For the moment, for a while, being twelve was not so bad, not bad at all, and Martha sensed that a whole other world lay beyond twelve. A world still out of reach, but growing nearer by the second.

"Okay," said Jimmy, the Benton house coming into view, "here's a question for you. Have you ever been kissed by a guy?"

Martha had never been so surprised by a question in her entire life. Her whole body went soupy, even her fingers and toes. She coughed. And choked on her cough. And coughed again.

"You okay?" asked Jimmy.

Martha nodded between coughs.

"You sure?"

Martha nodded again.

"Phew," said Jimmy. A smile rushed across his face. "That was close. No more questions." He pointed the tripod straight ahead. "I have a new tape. We've got filming to do."

40

Dream

Martha felt as though she had been plunged into a dream. She was living from moment to moment, without the certainty of what would happen next.

The sweater. A loose knot at the end of the stable. Martha spotted it immediately, as if it had been placed in the open, just waiting to be found. She pulled it on despite its slight dampness and took its quick discovery as a good omen.

Jimmy set up the tripod. He attached the camera and aimed it at Martha.

Martha disappeared into the stable. "Not scary in here during the day," she shouted. Sunlight came down in shafts. Dust motes floated in the air like tiny bubbles. Martha moved her arms in and out of the light. Stripes appeared (He loves me. . . .) and disappeared (He loves me not. . . .) on her sweater.

"Hey," yelled Jimmy, "what are you doing?"

"Nothing."

When Martha came out of the stable, at the very place she had entered it, Jimmy was there, and when she started walking toward the Benton house, he stopped her. "Stay here," he said.

"Huh?"

"Stay here." He put his hands on her shoulders and guided her, moving her a few feet to her left. "Right—here. Stop." He looked over his shoulder. "Good."

Now the dream intensified.

Time was magnified. Were his hands still on her shoulders? She couldn't say. His face swam up to hers. She grew extremely still. There was a flicker across his temple. The corners of her mouth twitched. Everything seemed to be tilting.

Now.

He.

Kissed.

Her.

41
A Bet

It—the kiss—was over in an instant, and yet Martha sensed she had skipped a few minutes of her life.

Jimmy drew away from her and made a thumbs-up sign. Then he pumped a fist. "I've got it!" he said.

Martha's eyes grew smaller as she tried to figure out what was happening.

"I've got it on film," said Jimmy, grinning, "and I won the bet."

His words and the look on his face caused a sudden, peculiar shift in Martha's feelings. Thoughts darted around her head like birds. "What?" she whispered.

"Our kiss," he said. "I've got it on film. You know, the tripod," he added, nodding, as if this explained everything. He ran to the camera and came right back. "It's turned off now," he said. "Don't worry."

Martha tried to stay calm. She held him in her stare for a long time, so long he started to blush and fidget.

"Well, the bet was nothing, really," he said. "Just a joke. I bet Vince and my brothers that I could get you to kiss me on video before they came back from sailing." He shrugged and reached out toward her. "And it'll be great for the love section of my film. That's why I did it. For the film."

Martha moved aside. "You are a—" she said, stopping because no word she knew was bad enough. She eked out an "Oh," before she raised her eyebrows in defeat, set her jaw, and fled.

"Lighten up!" Jimmy yelled to her back.

Martha only made it as far as the beech tree before she lost her composure. She fell against the smooth trunk and slid to the ground. Her entire life had come down to this awful moment, dwindled to nothing but this. Her life was a measly mess that could be contained in a closed fist. But her sadness could not be contained, and so she cried and cried.

42
Solidarity

After about thirty minutes had passed, Martha figured it was safe to walk back to Godbee's. There were no tears left in her, and she figured the telltale signs of crying would have disappeared by the time she got to her grandmother's house. If not, her puffy, bloodshot eyes and splotchy cheeks would surely elicit questions from her parents. The last thing she wanted. She willed herself to bluff cheeriness at all costs. Her only protection.

She decided she would never tell anybody what had happened. Ever. Even Godbee. But the problem with this plan was so obvious that when it dawned on Martha, about five seconds later, she felt a sudden loss of oxygen and felt stupid to her very core.

The tape existed. And since there had been a bet, the tape would be shown to Vince and Jimmy's brothers as proof. And who knew who else Jimmy would show his film to when he finished it?

Martha's stomach lurched. She became intensely aware of her separateness to the whole world. This wasn't exactly the right way to put it, because if she were truly separate from the whole world, she wouldn't care about the videotape; it would have no effect. She was mixed up—that's what she was. Miserably so.

She imagined a million puzzle pieces floating around inside her, all jumbled up. When (*if!*) all the puzzle pieces fit together, everything would be okay, all her problems would be solved, and she would have made it through this awful part of her life. If any of the pieces had previously been locked together, today's events had surely dislodged them. What had promised to be the best day of her life had become the worst.

She trudged on, her lips compressed, her face still slightly dappled. She had walked a good distance when Olive returned to her thoughts. She now felt a strange solidarity with Olive that went beyond the journal entry. She guessed that Olive would have known how she, Martha, felt at this very moment. How it felt to be tricked. Martha wondered what

Olive would have done in this situation. The glimpses Martha had seen of Olive at school led her to believe that she would have just ignored Jimmy, ignored the whole incident. Olive would have quietly proceeded with her life.

Maybe, thought Martha, just maybe, the kiss will never be mentioned and the tape never shown. Her mind circled back to this thought repeatedly, although deep down inside her, she knew the likelihood of this was next to impossible. She had seen the delight on Jimmy's face. So, because it was the best thing she could think of to do, Martha would pretend the kiss and the tape were meaningless. And if that didn't work, she would try to block this episode out of her life, let it become a blind spot, ignore it. Like Olive, she would quietly proceed with her life.

43

Great!

Pretending worked well for a very short time with her parents, Lucy, and Godbee. Martha tried to be the perfect, responsive, talkative but not too chatty, polite, eager twelve-year-old.

"Are you all right?" her father asked after a while, concern wrinkling his forehead.

"Fine. Fine." Perhaps she was overdoing it.

Then her mother asked, "So how was Mr. Jimmy Manning?"

"Great!" she answered. Her voice was over-enthusiastic and a tremor ran through it. She decided avoidance would be her best bet. She left the room quickly, little explosions going off inside her. She sat on the seawall and sucked her knuckles.

44

Hate

When Vince returned, Martha was still sitting on the seawall. She watched him grow from a dot to her brother, as if he were emerging from the water's frothy edge. The easygoing way he carried himself led Martha to believe that her brother's life was uncomplicated. As he drew near, he shrugged his backpack from his shoulder and swung it in a big circle around him, shifting it from hand to hand. He approached her with a flinty smile that softened as he got closer.

"Hi," he said.

She searched his face for clues. Found none. His face was both open and closed at the same time. "Hi," she replied in a measured tone.

Martha wanted to know what Vince knew. And she didn't want to know.

And she did.

And she didn't.

She slid off the seawall and stood before her brother, blocking his path. "I can read your mind," she said, giving him an opening.

"And it says?"

"You tell me."

Vince looked at her as if she were crazy. "It says you're a shitty mind reader. World's worst."

"Very funny. Tell me."

"Tell you *what*?" He seemed to be chewing back a grin.

"You know." Her eyes were slits. "I know you know."

"Then what's the point?" He tried to go around her, but she mirrored his move.

"Please?" she said.

He shook his head in disbelief. "Okay, okay—have it your way. I was just doing you a favor, you know. Trying to be a nice brother and not rub it in." His voice was self-important now. He brushed past her, using his backpack as a buffer between them. And as he did, he kissed the air twice. Noisily. Two big smooches. "There—are you happy now?"

Martha ripped the backpack from Vince's hand and threw it down. "I hate you."

"Me? What did *I* do? It wasn't my idea. *I* didn't kiss anybody."

"I hate you," Martha said again. "I really, truly hate you."

Clotted with anger, Martha only heard the first part of what Vince said next as he scooped up his backpack and walked to the house. "Yeah, well, I think you're—" he began.

"Yeah, well, I think you're—" she said, doing as cruel an imitation as possible. She felt lopsided, standing with one foot on a rock, slumping to one side like a misshapen statue.

45

Every Particle of a Thought

"I don't know what's going on between you and Vince—and I don't *want* to know—but I don't want a scene at dinner. Got it?"

"Yes," said Martha. Yes, Ms. Hubbard.

"Remember, when your father and I are dead and gone, your brother and sister will *be* your family."

Blah, blah, blah, blah, blah.

Martha ducked into the rental car (van, actually) and slid the door shut as hard as she could. She climbed to the back, next to Lucy, who had just been belted into her car seat and was squirming like a landed fish. Through the window, Martha watched her mother say something to Vince, watched Vince roll his eyes. He sat down on the middle seat, and Martha stared at the back of his head, pretending that every time she blinked invisible arrows pierced his scalp.

Under normal conditions she would have been tingling with anticipation. They were going to her favorite restaurant, right on the water in Woods Hole. And although she would order what she always ordered—deep-fried shrimp on a roll with coleslaw and fries and lots of ketchup on the side—the grip of unhappiness over the kiss would be too strong for her to enjoy the meal.

While she toyed with her food, her mind grew alert, picking up every particle of a thought and magnifying it, letting it expand and become huge and always ending with Jimmy Manning and shame. Even something as innocuous as a french fry (french fry—ketchup—red—heart—valentine—kiss—Jimmy Manning) had weight and meaning and was ominous.

From behind Martha, harsh, low sunlight fell over the table like a net. The lid from one of Lucy's jars of baby food gleamed.

"You're awful quiet." The comment came from her father out of nowhere. "Silenced by the charms of Jimmy Manning?" He suppressed a look of amusement.

Martha responded with a stiffened back and a bunched face. If she wasn't careful, she knew tears would rise up.

"Jimmy Manning," said Vince, wrinkling his nose ever so slightly, "Jimmy Manning can be a prick."

"Vincent," said his father. "We don't need talk like that. I'm sure your grandmother doesn't appreciate it."

"I'd appreciate some more coleslaw," Godbee said. "That's what I'd appreciate."

As Godbee extended her hand across the table to receive a bowl of coleslaw from her son, Martha's eyes caught Vince's. She almost smiled at him. And he almost smiled back.

Dusk. The moon looked like a chalk smudge. Someone—a boy—was sitting on Godbee's stoop. He rose as the van approached, then he sat down again, rose once more, walked down the steps, then back up them, moving as if in a dream's slow motion.

The storm in Martha's chest turned to stone. Oh, God, she thought, it's him.

But it wasn't. It was Tate, and he wanted to talk to Martha. She led him along the seawall away from her family, away from her father's voice and the only word she could make out: "intrigue." Lights in the house flipped on.

"What is it?" asked Martha quietly.

"Um," said Tate. "I, um . . ."

Despite the darkening sky, she could see his eyes. There was a sadness to them, and an intensity. And he was fidgety. Martha had no idea what he wanted. Suddenly it struck her that Tate always seemed to be around, often on the fringes, but always there, like a shadow.

Tate lifted his eyebrows. "I'm sorry about what my brother did to you. The bet, I mean." He paused. "He thinks he's so great." Another pause. "I didn't know what to do." Another. "That's it, I guess." When he finished, his mouth was little more than a slanted line. He started to walk away. He was shaking his head.

"I didn't know what to do." The words implied to Martha that Jimmy had been using her all along, that maybe he had never liked her at all, and his saying "I need you" right before he had taken her hand as they walked on the beach was a lie. Still, part of her wanted to believe it: "I need you." She had, for once, however briefly, felt needed for something other than baby-sitting or loading the dishwasher or helping her father fix dinner.

"Really," Tate said, stopping. "I didn't—I didn't know what to do," he repeated without turning around.

Martha drew a deep breath. Let it out. She felt inadequate and foolish, but she also stole some confidence from Tate's uncomfortable manner. "Well, maybe next time you'll know what to do," she called after him.

A minute passed. Tate had faded into the night.

"Thank you," whispered Martha.

47

Whirlwind in a Kitchen

Martha peeked into the kitchen. Godbee was alone, hunched forward over the sink, at work.

"Will you play?" asked Martha, holding up the Parcheesi box. Her invitation was accompanied by an uncertain smile.

Godbee turned. "Of course," she said. She had brought Lucy's empty baby food jars home from the restaurant and was rinsing them out. On the counter, the row of empty, clean jars was growing. "You know, darling, we haven't had our sharing session yet today."

Martha swallowed. "I know," she said tentatively. She had only one thing left worth telling—the kiss—and she couldn't do it; she couldn't bear to talk about it. "I just don't know what—"

"Hey, I'll play," said Vince, blasting into the kitchen.

"Sure," said Martha, relieved.

"Set up the game," said Godbee.

"I'll watch," said Martha's mother, suddenly materializing at Martha's shoulder. She stroked her daughter's hair, then whispered into her ear. "Do you want to talk? Just us?"

Martha pressed a fingertip to the spot on her neck where she had felt her mother's breath. She shook her head definitively. No.

"I wanna play!" It was Lucy, racing to the table and grabbing the edge with both hands.

"You're too little," said her father. He was a few steps behind Lucy. The newspaper under his arm was falling out in sections. "Come back here, Lucy. Let's go look at those rocks and shells you collected."

Martha was getting the board ready. "I want blue," she said.

"I'm green," said Vince.

"Mine!" shouted Lucy.

"I'll get potato chips," said Vince.

Chair legs scraped against the floor. A cupboard door slammed shut. Lucy circled and shrieked. Martha's father slipped on the newspaper, tearing it. Dice rolled off the tabletop and clattered across the linoleum.

The room was buzzing, crammed with

people and movement and noise, and Martha hoped that everything that was filling the kitchen would push everything else out of her head.

48

Later

Later, in bed, Martha flounced about, unable to sleep. She snapped on the bedside light and tried to continue Olive's story but found it too painful. She flipped to a clean page in the middle of her notebook and managed to write the following:

Notes for later—Olive finally realizes that James is really a stupid, flat-faced boy with dull, dark blond hair and pink skin and with a brain and heart the size of a microbe.*

*(Microbe—use this word specifically. Microbes cause disease.)

Later still, in the middle of the night, Martha just had to get out of bed. As quietly as possible, she slipped through the sleeping house. As if by a magnet, she was pulled down to the kitchen.

A band of amber light leaked out from beneath the closed kitchen door. Slowly Martha swung the door open.

Godbee. She looked like a ghost of herself. She was dressed all in white: white nightgown, flimsy white bathrobe, white satin slippers; and the dimmed hanging light behind her made a nimbus around her head.

"Hi," Martha whispered.

Godbee was standing by the table, drying her hands vigorously in a towel. "Oh, sweetie, you're up late." She glanced at the brass clock above the door. "Or should I say early?"

"Can't sleep."

"Me neither. But I thought it was a curse of old age, not youth."

Martha shrugged. "Dad always says I have an old soul."

"He should know."

Martha crossed the room, joining Godbee at the table. Finished with the towel, Godbee folded it and draped it over the top rung of the nearest chair. Suddenly Godbee's hands, which had been hidden by the towel, were revealed to Martha. Martha gasped. "Oh, my God, what happened?"

"Oh, this? This is just food coloring." Godbee laughed silently and spread her fingers for Martha to see. Her crepey, knotted hands looked sallow and horribly bruised. They were stained red, blue, purple, and yellow. "If you didn't know the truth, I can see where you'd think something hideous had happened. I'll make sure I explain it to your father first thing in the morning, before he calls nine-one-one."

"What were you doing?" asked Martha, inclining her head.

"Ah, I'll show you."

Martha followed Godbee to the counter on the other side of the room.

"Look," said Godbee, sweeping her arm in

an arc toward the two windows by the sink.

"The baby food jars," said Martha.

"You can't get the proper effect now, in the dark, but tomorrow, during daylight, the sun will make them glow, and it will filter through them and—I hope—send colors all around."

Not all, but most of the baby food jars had been used by Godbee. She had filled them with water. The water had been tinted with food coloring. The jars sat on the window sills and on the upper ledges of the window sashes. Martha thought of stained glass and pictured rainbows all over the kitchen—walls, ceiling, countertops.

"Kind of a silly thing to do, I suppose," said Godbee, her eyes shining above her glasses, "but it'll be pretty, I think."

"It's not silly," said Martha. "What gave you the idea?"

"Come," said Godbee. "I need to sit down."

Gingerly they pulled out chairs and sat at the table.

"The idea," Godbee began, her voice low, "came to me in a dream."

Martha listened, her mouth pursed in concentration, her chin tucked into her fists.

"I've had a recurring dream," Godbee

explained, "in which I'm standing on a beach. I'm a young girl. Naked. The waves are coming in, cresting before me, splashing my legs. But, oddly, there is no sound. Each wave is a color—red, purple, pink, apricot, blue, electric green—and the colors repeat. The waves swell, rise higher and higher. I get pulled out to sea, but I'm not frightened. I stay on top of the water, almost floating, riding the waves, curled up like a shrimp. The sun shines through the water, and the colors are brilliant.

"Then I travel downward through the water. The colors are layered now, horizontal, like stripes. Shadows flicker. I sink deeper and deeper, watching my skin change color . . ." Her voice trailed off.

"Then I always wake up," said Godbee. She blinked owlishly.

Martha looked at her arms and imagined what they would look like in Godbee's dream.

Godbee said, "I must have been thinking about the dream and about my story of the girl who moved away from the ocean. Hence, the bottles of colored water."

"The girl who saved the ocean in a bottle," said Martha.

"Idle thoughts," said Godbee. "Oh, dear . . ."

Silence fell between them. Martha yawned. Godbee's breathing thickened.

After a minute, Godbee changed the subject. "Seeing as it's after midnight," she said, "you could tell me *two* things. We need to make up for yesterday."

Martha shrugged uncomfortably, pinching her neck with her shoulders. Her eyes stung.

"What is it?" asked Godbee.

"I guess . . . I don't know . . . I'm kind of worn out of telling you about me." Martha's voice was threaded with hesitancy. She shifted about on her chair. "Can I not tell you about me anymore? Is that okay?"

"Oh, sweetie. Of course. I didn't mean for this to be work."

But there was something Martha wanted to know. Some advice she needed. "But can I ask you something?"

"Yes."

"What do you do when you're really, really sad?" When you're full of dread, is what she really meant.

Godbee exhaled through her nose, making a whistling sound. "Hmm. When I'm genuinely suffering, I try to think of someone worse off than I am. And then, if it happens to be someone I know and I'm feeling particularly saintly, I try to do something nice for him or her." After a beat, she placed the back of her hand on her forehead and cocked her head toward the ceiling. "Oh, dear, listen to your grandmother blather." She waved her words aside.

It was quiet. Martha sniffed and gazed off. She yawned again. Then she played with her hands. Studied them until they became unfamiliar. The puckers of skin at her knuckles, the little pale hairs, the tracery of veins—all these things grew ugly before her eyes. Old.

"Beautiful," said Godbee absently. "Your hands are seventy years younger than mine."

Martha let the focus of her eyes go soft. And then something occured to her. She felt it like a charge. "Godbee?" she said. "Can I have one of the empty jars? Please? One you didn't use."

Godbee nodded.

Martha thanked her grandmother and hugged her. She chose a jar from among those left on the counter. Then, hardly able to hold up her head, she shuffled off to bed, bleary eyed, carrying the empty jar as if it were a rare shell.

50
Confirmed

Before going down to breakfast the next morning, Martha reread the journal page from Olive, memorizing part: *I also hope that one day I can go to a real ocean such as the Atlantic or Pacific.*

Doing this confirmed Martha's idea. She now had something with which to combat the burden of her mood.

51

Lellow

"Lellow is best," said Lucy.

"Yellow," Martha corrected.

"Lellow," said Lucy, nodding.

Martha smiled. "Right."

"Looks like piss to me," said Vince, grinning.

The little glass jars in the kitchen windows shone like jewels.

"It's not as grand as I had hoped it would be," said Godbee, "but it's nice."

After breakfast, Martha toyed with a few of the jars. When she placed them on the table in direct sun, the jars sparkled. Arrows of light shot out of them, and the shadows cast by the jars were pools of color.

"Pretty," said Lucy. She grabbed at them greedily.

Martha slowed her sister down. She plopped Lucy onto her lap and watched over her patiently. "Be careful," Martha warned, guiding Lucy's hands, "they're Godbee's."

"I forgot something," said Lucy, turning around. She reached for and held Martha's face and gave her her usual morning kiss, getting it right on the first attempt. "Good one," said Lucy.

"I've been kissed," said Martha playfully. Instantly the meaning of the statement changed and deepened. And so did the color of Martha's cheeks.

52
Bulge

Martha and Lucy were still at the kitchen table when their father poked his head into the room and said, "Vince and I are going to walk over to the Benton place. Just snoop around. Any takers?"

Martha knew that if she said no, she might very well get stuck watching Lucy. "No," she said anyway. "I'd rather stay here." She wondered if she'd ever allow herself to go to the Benton place again.

"Me, too," said Lucy.

"Okay," said their father. He stepped onto the threshold and put his hands on both sides of the door frame, filling the space. He looked right at Martha. "Well, then, will you keep an eye on Lucy? We'll be back in about an hour or so."

Martha nodded.

"Mom should be done soon, and Godbee's still gabbing."

Godbee was having tea with her friend

Mrs. Maxwell in the living room. Martha's mother had needed to make a few calls for work. She was upstairs talking on her cell phone.

Martha went to the opened window in the hallway off the kitchen and watched her father and brother trudge through the sand. They appeared to be laughing. For some reason, she found this upsetting, as if she had been shut into an empty room, alone. She felt jealous, and then silly for feeling so, and then was baffled by how changeable and brief her feelings could be. Glued to the window, she pressed her forehead to one of the panes of the raised sash and lightly touched her fingertips to the screen below.

"Come back," Lucy demanded, breaking the trance Martha had slipped into.

"Yes, your majesty," said Martha. "I know— let's go outside, Lucy-poo."

"No," said Lucy.

It was a bit of a challenge, but Martha coaxed Lucy away from the jars in the kitchen and down to the beach.

Martha carried Lucy on her back to the inlet just south of Godbee's. Still, shallow

water, forgotten by the main current, surrounded a small, rippled sandbar. Slowly,
steadily, the tide was going out.

Martha had purposely worn her jeans and,
of course, one of her orange T-shirts,
untucked. The T-shirt easily covered the bulge
in her front pocket. The bulge was the empty
baby food jar. Martha willed it not to break.

Martha wanted privacy when she carried out the first part of her plan, so she talked Lucy into being buried in the sand.

Lucy was perfectly happy, covered up, motionless except for her head, which she turned from side to side, and her wiggly fingers and toes, which caused little earthquakes.

"You're like a big turtle on its back," said Martha, patting down and smoothing the mound that held her sister secure. Martha noticed that Lucy's beautiful hair was gritty with sand but said nothing, to avoid a tantrum. "Okay," Martha said, "you're a . . . you're a princess who's been put under a paralyzing spell. To break the spell, I need to get a magic potion or a magic stone from the sea. So stay here and don't move, and when I come back I'll free you."

Lucy squealed with delight.

"I shall return, fair princess," Martha

exclaimed, deepening her voice in a comical fashion and arching her eyebrows.

With her pants legs rolled up, Martha waded across the near end of the inlet and stepped onto the sandbar. She glanced over her shoulder to check on Lucy. Quickly she strode across the little island to its farthest point. She retrieved the jar from her pocket, knelt, and in one swift, seamless movement, filled the jar with water from the bay. She replaced the lid and screwed it on tightly.

Olive, this is for your mother, Martha thought. This is because you never made it to an ocean.

Martha held the jar up to the light and squinted. The water in the jar was speckled with motes, teeming with microscopic life. She felt so good about her idea, her heart expanded. She felt oddly buoyant. She would bring the jar home to Wisconsin and give it to Olive's mother. A memorial from the sea.

Martha didn't know where Olive's mother lived, but finding out that piece of information should prove easy enough, she thought. She could look in the parents' handbook from school.

The jar seemed to take on weight in Martha's hand as it took on importance in her mind.

For a few minutes, Martha had forgotten about Lucy, and when she remembered, she gently shoved the jar into her pocket, spun around, and ran in her sister's direction.

Martha stopped. Jimmy Manning was walking down the beach, coming her way. He was holding his video camera with one hand and holding the hand of a girl Martha had never seen before with the other.

She didn't know what to do, how to avoid him, how to remain unseen. She could stand still, frozen like a pole, and most likely be spotted. Or? Casting about with her eyes, she saw no exit. She turned on her heel and walked, with her head down, back out to the end of the sandbar. When she reached the end, she stole a peek behind her. They were still approaching. Laughing. Swinging arms.

Martha took one step into the water. Another step. Her next step found no footing. The sandbar had disappeared. She fell, slipping into the sea with barely a sound.

54

Sea Creature

She had only meant to wait it out, wait unnoticed until *he* had passed, taking baby steps, wanting to disappear, but then she actually *did* disappear, dropping into the water that was everywhere—no sides no top no bottom—and taken so by surprise that it didn't matter that she was close to shore or that she was a good swimmer because she panicked and in her panic she swallowed water and scratched her cheek and somehow clawed her hair loose from its ponytail and her hair spread out from her head like a multitude of tentacles thin as filaments like a sea creature jerking about wildly and then for a second she felt numb and blue and liquid herself and resigned to the fact that the water would overcome her and in that second she began sliding away from the present and she stopped thrashing about and relaxed and felt like a bird caught in a draft of air rather than a girl pushed and pulled by the ocean and gave up.

I'm drowning, she thought, and it was the very thought that made her kick and stroke and kick and stroke until she broke through the surface of the water and made her way back to shore oh so happy to be alive and coughing and coughing and coughing.

55
Change

The world can change in a minute, and at the same time remain unchanged. Martha's incident in the ocean had lasted no longer than that—a minute. Martha, gulping air, her chest heaving, realized that, in one way, during that time, the world hadn't changed a bit—Lucy was still as happy as could be, exactly where she had been left, and Jimmy Manning and the girl had passed by, oblivious. But, in another way, the world had changed dramatically— because Martha understood for the first time that the world didn't revolve around her, that it was bigger than that, that it simply *was*, and would continue to exist with or without her. But she was here, and wanting to be, more than ever.

I could've drowned, she thought.

She shivered. Her nose and throat burned. Her ears pulsed. Forgetting that she was soaked to her skin, Martha wiped her hands on her pants to dry them. That's when she felt and remembered the jar. She pulled it out of her pocket and held it in her open hand. It was a glorious thing.

Lucy was pretending to be asleep—an impossible task. She opened her eyes wide, looked at Martha, looked away quickly, giggled, fought to close her eyes, succeeded for a moment, then started over again.

When her breathing calmed, Martha flopped down beside Lucy, placing the jar on the ground, turning it like a screw safely into the sand. She rose on one elbow above her sister. She didn't care that sand was sticking to her all over.

"I nearly drowned to save you, your majesty," Martha whispered into the pink whorl of Lucy's ear.

"Yourm blooding," said Lucy. "Is it magic?"

"What?"

"Your cheek," said Lucy.

Martha sat and brought her hand up to her face. Her fingers found the scratch. Then she looked at her fingers. A smear of blood. She let out a quick, blithe laugh. "Oh, this is nothing, your majesty. A small price to pay for conquering an evil sea creature."

Lucy's eyes were marbles, big ones.

Martha's hair was plastered to her head and still dripping. She held a clump of hair over Lucy and wrung it out. Drips landed on the sand mound. "Now you are free," said Martha. "The spell is broken. You may go live your life, safe from harm. Prosper," she added, extending her arms, inviting her sister to get up.

Lucy erupted from the sand as if she were emerging from an egg, slowly at first, then in one big burst. She shook her arms and stretched her fingers. She gamboled in a circle. Within seconds, she realized that sand was under her shirt and pants, inside her diaper, in her hair, and so, announced her sudden discomfort to the world by stopping abruptly, making fists, drawing a breath, and producing one of her ear-piercing cries.

Unfazed, Martha grabbed Olive's jar and grabbed Lucy. She alternated between walking fast and jogging back to the house. She was humming softly to herself. Her jeans felt tight and cold, the creases sharp with sand. The fishy ocean breeze chilled her to the bone. She hurried, partly because of that; partly because of her shrieking, writhing sister; and partly because of her secrets and random thoughts, which carried her along and caused her to swell with happiness, or the expectation of it.

I did something good for Olive.

Tate is kind of nice.

I love Godbee.

Lucy's cheeks are perfect.

I almost drowned, but I didn't.

I'm alive.

56

A Note

Martha and Lucy reached the house. Martha was wondering how to handle Lucy now, what her strategy should be, when, to her relief, their mother flung open the screen door. "Is she okay? Are you okay?" she asked, stepping outside and taking Lucy into her arms.

"I think she's upset because she's got sand all over her. Inside and out."

"What about your cheek?"

"What? Oh, I scratched it trying to shoo a bug. Dumb." Martha looked down at her right hand; her left hand still clutched the small jar. "I guess my fingernails are longer than usual." How lame, she thought. But she was slightly amazed at how easily the words had come to her.

Their mother soothed Lucy, bouncing and swaying and talking to her in a rapid singsong. "You're fine. You're fine and fine and fine . . ." Lucy quieted and their mother grew still. "And you're *soaked*," she said to Martha as though this fact had just caught her attention. "What were you doing?" She started bouncing and swaying again.

"Oh, nothing," Martha replied. "I was just goofing around. I fell into the water on purpose to try to get Lucy to laugh. Didn't work."

She suspected that Lucy was still too self-absorbed at the moment—nuzzling into their mother's neck—to contradict her or to proclaim Martha a liar.

"This sand is insidious," said their mother, brushing at Lucy's shirt with the back of her hand. Let's take this all off." She unsnapped Lucy's shirt and pants and tugged and pulled at them, working them off while still holding her. She shook the clothes out and hung them on the doorknob. "We'll get you a new outfit, Miss Lucy. And, you, Martha, you should shower and get some dry clothes on." She paused; her cheeks were suddenly touched with pink—bright, uneven patches like those a child draws on a face with a crayon. "And, you know, you're so patient with her. You'll make a good mother someday."

Usually a remark like that would have caused Martha to seethe and feel as though acid were coursing through her veins, heading straight to her heart to shrivel it. But, surprisingly, it didn't affect her that way now. She smiled tightly but pleasantly, her lips together, a combination of self-respect and self-consciousness. With downcast eyes, she watched her mother go into the house.

That's when she noticed the piece of paper sticking out from beneath the doormat. Her mother's bare foot had been right on it, covering it. She pulled the paper out from under the mat. It was folded in half and in half once more, and taped shut. Martha's name was printed on the outside in small block letters. The handwriting was unfamiliar.

She turned the paper over and over in her hand. The paper was cream colored and textured, the ink blue. She glanced around. No one was in sight. She broke the seal and unfolded the paper.

The note said:

> *Martha—*
> *I think I know what to do.*
> *You'll see.*
> 　　　　　*—Tate*

The minutes accumulated. Martha sat on the stoop, trying to figure out the meaning of the message.

57
Scratch

Martha showered until the steam in the narrow stall enveloped her like curtains of thick fog. Wrinkled, dressed, exhausted, exhilarated, she wandered throughout the house. Twice she checked the doormat for another note. None appeared.

Godbee asked about the scratch on her cheek. So did her father. Martha lied automatically.

She examined the scratch in the hallway mirror. It was nothing, really. A two-inch red line angled up from her nostril on her right cheek, scabbing over on the end near her ear. When she looked closely, she saw traces of blue in her skin surrounding it.

She raised her hand to the scratch. She softly patted it, and then began patting her other cheek with her other hand as though she were putting in order all the thoughts inside her head.

The afternoon passed, and the night, and the next morning—all uneventful. The words from Tate's note kept running through Martha's mind like music. If it preoccupied her, it was not in a bad way. In fact, since falling into the ocean, what she saw or experienced or felt was done so through a filter, a filter that made everything more bearable, understandable, acceptable.

Martha had put the note from Tate, the small jar of seawater, and the page from Olive's journal under her bed in the canary yellow room, pushing them as far back as possible into the dusty darkness, making sure in the morning that the bedspread was pulled down, keeping her treasures hidden.

She had abandoned her story about Olive, convinced that it was not very good, nor worthy of Olive. But she knew that she wanted to be a writer more than ever. She held on to this feeling without trying to start a new novel just yet. She decided she would try a poem instead—the best poem ever—reasoning that it would be easier to write and to finish, only to discover that this was difficult as well. She ended up with a page of first lines.

The ocean like a big blue overcoat zippered
    me up
The ocean is full of tears, you know
Under the sea I lived
I was a sea creature for one moment
If I had died beneath the waves
My grandmother dreamed of the ocean
Can you put the sea in a bottle, keep it?
Can you watch a hand grow old?
Why did one girl die and not the other?
Save me, oh save me, so I do not drown
A girl with one kiss equals an ocean of tears
I kissed a stone and thought to drown
Who is this boy who left me a note?
You are always there like the sea or sky or air
Meet me at the seawall, salt on your toes,
    waiting

After rereading her hour's worth of work, she thought she wouldn't try to write anything else until she was back home in Wisconsin. She shoved her notebook under the bed so that all of her possessions that mattered were together. Safe.

59
Formless Days

Martha felt like a jar brimming with secrets. No one knew about Olive or the note from Tate or that she had nearly drowned. She wanted it that way.

There were Jimmy and the kiss and the video, too, of course, but those things weren't secrets. Not completely, anyway. Another secret: Martha found herself caring less and less about Jimmy and thinking more and more about Tate.

She wondered if the video would ever be erased from her memory, wondered if she'd ever ask Vince what the video was actually like, what she looked like in it. She doubted it.

She wondered if she'd still remember this particular summer when she was Godbee's age, if she lived that long. And she wondered if Godbee could remember being twelve.

Should she call Tate? Stop by his house? After what had happened with Jimmy, she was hesitant. She'd wait. And she didn't have long to do so—only two full days remained before she would return home.

And they turned out to be formless days. Days in which she stayed close to Godbee's house (baking a peach pie with Godbee, weeding the garden, playing Parcheesi) or went on short sight-seeing trips with her family. Vince joined them on the trips and hung around the house, too, which surprised Martha.

"What about—your friends?" Martha asked him as they rode in the van to the Knob at Quissett Harbor. She had chosen her words carefully and had braced herself a little.

"I'm kind of tired of Jimmy. All he wants to do is play with his stupid video camera. It's boring."

They looked at each other for a long, long moment, and Martha was aware of the weight of things left unspoken.

"What about Tate?" she asked finally.

"He's okay. Kind of quiet."

At the Knob, Godbee stayed in the van with the door open to catch the breeze. "I've seen it," she said, motioning them on, the veins running along the back of her hand like rivers on a map. "Enchanting as it is, I've seen it."

Martha thought she could never see the Knob enough. It was just a little chunk of scrubby land, rimmed in rocks, jutting out into the bay, but it seemed magical to her, as if a precise and charming illustration from the endsheets of a book of fairy tales had been made real.

The water was silvery, the sky the same. A handful of people ambled about, some with walking sticks and binoculars.

Martha ran up the path, found the approximate center of the Knob, and turned around completely, her arms outstretched. You can see forever, she thought. She worried a rock with the toe of her shoe. She trailed her fingers along a length of barnacled driftwood. She pressed her lips together and let her vision blur, slowly slipping away, leaving her family and the other tourists behind without moving an inch. Deserting everyone. Except Tate.

Tate: "Hi. I thought you might be here."

Martha: "I love it here."

Tate: "Me, too."

Martha: "Yeah."

Tate: "Of course!"

Martha: "What?"

Tate: "It makes sense that we'd both love it here. Soul mates, you know."

Martha: "Right."

Tate: "There's something I have to tell you."

Martha: "Hmm?"

Tate: "I like—like you."

Martha: "Me, too."

"'Me, too,' what?" said her father.

Martha reddened. She shrugged and smiled. "Me *two*. Me *three*. Me *four*," she said, thinking quickly.

"You're a goofball," he said playfully.

On the drive home they passed mansions under construction near beautiful marshes.

"This is so awful," said Martha's mother. "Soon there won't be any cape left to ruin."

And then it happened again. Martha leaned against the window and looked past the trees and houses into the distance.

Martha: "Did you know I almost drowned?"

Tate: "Really?"

Martha: "Uh-huh."

Tate: "I almost did, too, once."

Martha: "Really?"

Tate: "Yeah."

Martha: "Mine happened this trip. When was yours?"

Tate: "I was ten. It was nothing, really."

Martha: "Tell me."

Tate: "No, you first. *You* tell *me*. Yours is more important. Totally. Tell me all about it. Every detail."

And she did.

And then, before she knew it, they were back at Godbee's and Tate was gone.

60

A Telephone Call

Sadness filled the house. Like a storm brewing, the feeling mounted for Martha as the day wore on. It was the last day, the last night of the trip. Everything took on a gloomy significance: the Last Lunch, the Last Dinner, the Last Sunset. The sadness was the familiar going-home-lump-in-your-throat feeling.

After dinner, Martha stared out the front window. There was a presence behind her. A tap on her shoulder.

"Honey," said Godbee. "The telephone is for you."

Martha raced to the phone. She hadn't even heard it ring. The receiver lay on the table next to the back door. She picked it up with both hands as if it were a large knobbed whelk. "Hello?" she said.

"Hi, um—Martha, this is Tate." His voice was wobbly.

"Hi."

"When are you leaving? Going home, I mean."

"Tomorrow. But not at the crack of dawn or anything. We have a later flight. My dad wants to leave here by ten o'clock at the latest."

"Okay. That's good. Ten o'clock. Tomorrow. Um—bye."

"Wait. Are you coming over?" Her voice faltered a little.

"Yes," was the reply. And then he quickly hung up before she could ask when.

61

Bad Dream

When?

That was the question. Martha was still asking it as she climbed the stairs, very late, to go to bed.

She had done most of her packing; she'd finish in the morning. The note, the journal page, the jar of water, and her notebook were now in her backpack. The backpack was tucked under the bed. Mindful of the fragility of the jar of water, she had wrapped it in one of her dirty T-shirts and bound it with a huge rubber band. Martha had seen the rubber band, one of many, hanging from a nail in the pantry. When she had asked Godbee if she could have it, Godbee had said, "Take whatever you want."

Martha lay in bed. On her stomach. On her back. On one side. On the other.

When? When? When?

During one of their talks, Godbee had offhandedly said, "We all trail complications."

At the time, Martha had thought that Godbee had been referring to Martha's father. For some reason the remark circled in Martha's thoughts until she fell asleep.

Toward dawn, she dreamed.

She dreamed she was in a silent room filled with what appeared to be large blocks of ice, spaced evenly throughout, in rows. Some were her height; some were taller. They were as deep and wide as dressers. They had rounded edges. The positioning of the ice blocks seemed planned, perfectly ordered, and yet Martha sensed that there was something terribly wrong, some hidden danger.

As she walked among the blocks, she reached out, touching one tentatively, expecting to find it cold and hard. Surprisingly, it was warm and pliable. There was movement, ever so slightly, from within. The movement gradually became more pronounced.

Abruptly, and with great clarity, she understood her surroundings. The blocks were actually thick plastic bags enclosing people, people trying to escape. Her mother was encased in one. So was her father. Lucy. Vince. Jimmy. Tate. All the Mannings. Godbee, too.

Godbee was trapped in the nearest one, clawing madly. Her rapid, frantic breathing fogged the plastic. Her wide, terrified eyes appeared and disappeared behind the clouded barrier.

Desperately Martha tried to release her grandmother—pulling, punching, poking— with no success. At last she saw a clear zipper, nearly invisible, at the back of the plastic bag and yanked it down. Relieved, she blinked, then looked upward, expectantly, only to find that Godbee had vanished.

The dream ended.

Martha woke thickheaded. The residue from the bad dream lingered until she remembered the question.

When?

62

Brave

Seven o'clock.

Eight o'clock.

Nine o'clock.

And still no sign of Tate.

I could have drowned, Martha reminded herself, as a way to alleviate her disappointment, trying to assume the role of what her mother would call a "trouper."

Martha's suitcase and backpack had already been gathered up by her father and added to the other luggage amassing outside by the van. She sat alone on the edge of her bed, an island, her feet dangling, her arms at her sides stiff as branches. What she wanted was to stop time. If she held her breath and froze completely, could she make it happen? Periodically, something—a door slamming, Vince pounding down the stairs, Lucy crying—pierced the bubble that had formed around her.

"You really should eat something," her

mother called from the doorway, piercing the bubble again.

"Not hungry," Martha replied without turning around.

Minutes later, another interruption, a quiet one—Godbee entered the room, her slippers making a soft shushing sound on the worn wooden floor.

Martha turned, guessing correctly who it was approaching her. "I had a scary dream about you last night," she murmured.

"Do you want to tell me about it?" Godbee's voice was so strong compared to Martha's.

Martha shook her head; she didn't want to frighten Godbee or upset her. "It's too creepy. I think it meant that I don't want to go home."

"Good-byes are hard, aren't they?"

Martha nodded.

Godbee walked around the bed and sat down next to Martha. She held something in her hand—a folded piece of paper or a letter or a card of some sort.

The little bed squeaked and sagged. Granddaughter and grandmother sank into the mattress and into each other, their sides pressing together. Martha could feel the boni-ness of Godbee.

"Look at this," said Godbee. "I found it this morning while I was going through some papers with your father." She gave Martha the thing she had been holding. "I always knew you were brave."

"Me? Brave? Hardly."

"Look. You always were."

"What is it?"

It was a greeting card printed with an image of three cherubs riding a colorful fish underwater.

"Open it," said Godbee.

"Oh," said Martha. "*I* wrote this? How funny. I must have only been six or seven, or something."

The handwritten note inside the card said:

Dear Godbee,

I like to be at your house best of all. I like to climb on the stoney rocks down at the beach. I am a relly brave girl. I like to pretend I'm on a boat on rough water thats sinking.

Love,

Martha

"I can't remember this at all," said Martha, closing the card and running her finger over the striped body of the fish.

"See?" said Godbee. "You are brave. And you always were." She said it with such tenderness, and then she added, "Being brave was the one thing I always wanted to be and never thought I was." She placed one of her hands at the base of her throat.

"Really? Even now?"

"Now more than ever," Godbee said, looking at Martha steadily. Her face broke into a thin smile that seemed weary to Martha.

Martha smiled back primly. Another confession, another fact, another secret. And it stunned Martha more than the other things Godbee had told her. It didn't feel good to think of Godbee other than the way Martha had thought of her since she, Martha, was little. Godbee—strong, smart, pretty, loving, happy, polite, elegant, protective, nice, safe, and, yes, brave.

If you didn't get to be brave by the time you were Godbee's age, when would you?

What if this *was* their last summer together?

Quiet. A torrent of light was coming through the uncurtained window and, in the silence, seemed to have as much presence as sound.

For a reason she couldn't have explained, Martha wanted the card, but she could tell that Godbee was showing it to her, not giving it away. Martha handed it back to Godbee reluctantly.

"Maybe *this* will make me brave," said Godbee. She kissed the card and held it against her chest for a moment. "Oh, dear, it's almost time to leave," she said, "and I'm not one for long good-byes in public. So let's have our real good-bye now."

Martha let herself be enfolded by Godbee. By her thin, but strong, grasshopper arms, her smell.

Godbee said, "Hug me, child," and "I do love you."

Martha could feel Godbee's breath on her ear, feel her cool, silky skin on her neck, feel a strand of her unpinned hair at the corner of her mouth.

Martha thought she'd break Godbee if she hugged her back as hard as she wanted to, but she was filled with such love and longing and happiness and sorrow (not bravery, definitely not bravery) that she grabbed her grandmother's shoulders and squeezed with all her might.

63
Leaving

Martha's father clapped his hands together once, making a loud, crisp *smack*. "Time to go," he announced, one foot resting on the bumper of the van. "Van's loaded."

"But it's not ten o'clock yet," said Martha. "You told us we were leaving at ten o'clock." She looked down the beach in the direction of the Mannings' house, straining her eyes, waiting for Tate to materialize.

Her father glanced at his watch, a puzzled look distorting his face. "It's what—eight minutes to ten?" he said. "We're ready—let's go."

Vince was already in the van, buckled up, earphones in place, eyes closed, moving his head in a jerky rhythm. Godbee, Lucy, and Martha's mother were on the stoop. Martha's mother was holding Lucy, who was wiggling forward, holding on to Godbee's face, kissing it. Mrs. Maxwell had come to spend the morning with Godbee. She was inside, watching, visible through the front window like a portrait in a frame.

"I have to go to the bathroom," said Martha.

"Again?" said her father. "Hurry." He shook his head. "I hate traveling," he muttered.

Martha stalled as long as she could. She sat on the toilet, checking her watch. Still seated, she leaned toward the window and parted the curtains to keep an eye on what was happening outside.

Lucy was in her car seat now.

Her mother called, "Martha!"

Her father whistled for her—his ear-splitting whistle he only used when he meant business.

Martha ran downstairs and out to her family. She hugged Godbee one last time. A look passed between them. A meaningful silence. Their faces gave away their feelings.

When everyone was in the van with the doors closed, Martha's father started the engine, released the parking brake, and eased the van down the driveway. "We're off like a herd of turtles," he said, which is what he always said as they started out on a trip of any length.

All at once, Martha felt as though she were nothing and everything. She felt singular, in her sadness, and as common as a stone, too. She pictured the van as a container of disappointment, and she closed her eyes and settled back into her seat, fighting the thought that there is a possibility within each moment for change to occur, for good things to happen. Why bother? Perhaps she'd had enough things happen for one trip.

Behind closed eyelids, images of the past several days flashed. The kiss, Jimmy's film, lobsters, Parcheesi, Godbee's bottles of colored water, the bottle of water for Olive, Tate waiting, the late-night talk with Godbee, the Benton place, holding hands, Godbee's hands, dreams, Tate, the sea, the powerful powerful sea . . .

She opened her eyes to clear her head just as her father said, "Who *is* that?"

"Isn't it one of the Mannings?" said her mother.

Ten yards in front of them, in the middle of the road, waving his arms, was Tate.

Martha's heart jumped suddenly and rose like a leaf caught in a gust of wind. Then, just as quickly, her heart dropped. She didn't know what was going to happen. She was hoping it would be something good.

64
This Time

Was she witnessing some sort of miracle?

Martha's father pulled the van off the road onto the gravel shoulder.

It all happened so fast.

Tate ran over to the van, to the side where Martha was sitting. His eyes were wide and round. He had been motioning with one hand, drawing circles in the air, indicating that he wanted her to open the window. In his other hand he held a medium-size brown paper bag.

Martha slid the door open. The sun's harsh light was glaring from behind Tate, causing her to squint.

He was panting. He thrust the bag at her and said, "I knew what to do this time. It just took me this long to do it." A smile, pure and full and gleaming, spread across his face. "Phew—I made it." He let go of the bag. As he withdrew his hand, it touched her bare knee for seconds. His skin felt hot to her; his hand was burning. "Bye," he said, his eyebrows arched modestly. "You'll see me next time," he added, almost boldly, pulling away. "That's a promise."

Did she say thank you? Did she say goodbye?

That was it. She couldn't remember sliding the door shut, but she must have, because they were back on task, on their way to Providence and the airport.

"What is it?" asked Lucy.

"Nothing," Martha answered. And everything?

"I don't get it. He's not the one," she heard her father say.

"I guess he's the messenger. Who knows?" she heard her mother say.

"You are so behind," she heard Vince say, still bobbing his head.

They all must have said other things, but their voices were just part of the blurred background sounds.

She rolled and unrolled the top of the bag until the paper was soft and sweaty. But she wouldn't look inside. She lifted the bag off her lap to gauge its heft. Whatever was inside wasn't very heavy. She wanted to be alone

when she allowed herself to discover the contents of the bag.

She'd wait.

She'd wait until they were at the airport
and checked in and she could go to a rest room
alone and go into a stall and lock the door.

Which is exactly what she did.

A videotape was inside the bag, wrapped
hastily in newspaper. *The* videotape. A small
note was attached.

> *Here is the tape. See, I knew what to do*
> *this time.*
>
> *—Tate*
>
> *P.S. Jimmy will kill me when he finds out.*
> *P.P.S. I was the one who really liked you.*
> *P.P.P.S. Really.*

Martha put the tape in her backpack. She
took her time returning to her parents, sister,
and brother in the waiting area by their gate.
As she wove in and out of all the people—
rushing, talking, eating, laughing; some in
clumps, some alone—she realized that no one,
no one at all in the airport, or on the entire
planet for that matter, knew her thoughts,

knew what she was carrying inside her head and heart. And at that very minute, what was inside her head and heart made her feel as though there was no one else in the whole world she would rather be.

65

A String of Preparations

Home was the same as when Martha had left it, but because *she* had changed, her world seemed slightly different, as though she were seeing everything in sharper focus. She was glad to be in her own room, but the color of the walls (pale blue) and the pattern of the curtains (cherries, chosen after Vince had moved to his own room) had lost their appeal for her in the short time she'd been away. Her room could easily belong to Lucy, she decided.

After she dropped her dirty clothes down the laundry chute, Martha emptied the contents of her backpack onto her bed and organized it. Her parents were decent about privacy, so she didn't have to bury her things in the back corners of her closet, just place them in her bottom right desk drawer where they were hidden from plain sight but accessible.

The jar of water for Olive's mother had survived the trip beautifully. When Martha had unwrapped it, she half expected it to be cracked and empty, the T-shirt that protected it wet. She found it strange that something so insignificant—the jar—could contain a piece, however tiny, of something so grand—the ocean. Olive's ocean. That's what she now thought to call the jar of water. Olive's ocean.

Then there was the tape. On one hand, it was certain relief to own it. On the other hand, just looking at it—the black plastic case—brought back the sting of deep embarrassment like nothing else could. Tate had done a noble thing by giving her the tape, although she wished he had simply destroyed it himself and told her. She had no idea, yet, what to do with it. She was so conflicted about it. Watch it? Not? Throw it away? Smash it with a hammer? Save it for when she was Godbee's age, trying to remember what it was like to be twelve?

What to do with the tape was only one of many decisions she had to make. She'd been home only a couple of hours, and she should have been exhausted from traveling, but her head was spinning with all the plans that needed to be worked out. A string of preparations lay before her, giving her a sort of thrill, not pleasant, not unpleasant. She had so much to get ready for. . . .

School. What to do with the tape. How to thank Tate properly. How to keep in touch with him. She needed to call Holly. She still needed to tell her father she wanted to be a writer. She needed to find out where Olive's mother lived and deliver Olive's ocean. And, then, there was her biggest idea to prepare for. She had decided that she wanted to spend Christmas vacation at Godbee's. The idea had come to her in a brilliant burst of genius on the flight home.

It would be perfect—a week or ten days to be alone with Godbee, to keep a watchful eye on her, to take care of her; and time to be with Tate. ("I was the one who really liked you.")

Martha was certain that Godbee would be surprised and happy about a winter visit; the last several years she'd spent Christmas with Mrs. Maxwell and her extended family. It was Martha's parents who would need convincing. There was major groundwork to lay, strategies to figure out, but she had close to four months to do so. It would, most likely, be a difficult task, but it would be worth it. She would beg if she had to.

First things first, she thought. Before she went to bed, she'd try to call Holly. She'd look up Olive's mother's address in last year's parents' handbook from school. And she'd tell her father she wanted to be a writer.

66
Passing the Torch

Holly's line was busy, so Martha looked for and, after a great deal of searching, found, Olive's mother's address in the second semester amendment to the parents' handbook. She jotted down the address on a scrap of paper and slipped it into her pocket. According to the address, Olive's house was only six or seven blocks away. It's funny, Martha thought, that she lived so close and I never knew it.

Martha tried to call Holly again—still busy. She kept trying. A flicker of impatience shot through her. In the kitchen, she surveyed the paltry contents of the refrigerator, the telephone wedged between her shoulder and cocked head.

"Not much in there," said her father, crossing the room to where she stood. "I'll go shopping first thing in the morning." Because the refrigerator door was shielding Martha, he hadn't realized that she was using the telephone until he was right upon her. "Oops. Sorry," he mouthed.

Martha nodded. Still busy. "It's okay."

"Let me use the phone when you're finished," her father whispered.

"Done," said Martha, handing it over. She shut the refrigerator door with her foot, then walked over to the cupboards by the sink.

Martha didn't intend to eavesdrop, but she couldn't help herself, being right there, in the kitchen by her father, waiting to talk to him. She opened and closed a cupboard, rummaged through a drawer idly. She could tell he was speaking to an answering machine.

He said, "Hi, Phil, this is Dennis. We're home from my mother's. Give me a call and let me know when we can meet to talk about my coming back to the firm. Why don't we do lunch? Bye." He switched off the telephone and stood it up on the nearest counter. "It's been a long day," he said, turning toward Martha. "With any luck, your sister will sleep through the night."

Martha looked down, falsely absorbed, and traced circles around a knot in the wooden floor with her bare foot. Here's my chance, she thought. She raised her head. "Dad?"

"What, hon?"

"Can I ask you something?"

"Of course. Always."

"What about your job?"

"Well, I called Phil from Godbee's and told him I wanted to come back to the firm. We'll talk and see what works out. Things look good."

None of this truly mattered to her; she was leading up to what concerned her. She made her voice tentative. "That's—good."

"Don't worry about my job."

"I'm not. But—"

"But what?"

She passed her tongue across her teeth. "But will you miss being a writer?" There, she'd done it; she'd aimed their conversation in exactly the direction she'd wanted.

"Honey, I wasn't a writer. I *wanted* to be one and, who knows, maybe I'll try again some-day." He shrugged, then his tone changed, became playful, even goofy, clownish in his way that sometimes made Martha laugh and sometimes embarrassed her. Tonight she had neither reaction. "Listen, *you're* a fine writer," he told her. His face was shiny. His eyebrows wiggled. "*You* be the writer in the family." He tipped an imaginary hat her way.

"Really?" This was too easy.

"I'm kidding. You can be whatever you want to be."

"No, Dad, I *want* to be a writer."

"That's great." His tone had changed again. His voice was sincere and bright and made her ache just a little. "Great."

"You wouldn't care?" she asked, smiling self-consciously.

"Care? Of course not. I'm officially passing the torch." He bent down and lightly kissed the top of her head. "It's all yours."

4525 Nelson Street

Martha had slept soundly, woke refreshed, ate a quick breakfast, and took off on foot for Olive's mother's house. It was already hot outside and promised to get even hotter. It would be a steamy, sticky, slow-motion August day. After walking for mere minutes, tiny beads of perspiration formed on Martha's skin. She missed the cooling breeze from the sea.

Martha shifted the jar—Olive's ocean— from one hand to the other. She had memorized the address, and she repeated the number in her head like a chant. Forty-five twenty-five, forty-five twenty-five . . .

She was nearly there. She checked the number on each house. She was on the correct side of the street, just a couple of houses away.

There it was: 4525 Nelson Street. The house stood before her, up three shallow steps and a short length of sidewalk—a modest duplex, sided in white aluminum with a charcoal gray roof and a foundation of pale red bricks, almost pink. Little scrawny weed trees grew in the gutters in clumps. Fiery geraniums grew in pots hanging from both the front and side porches. Garbage—cans, bags, and loose piles—was heaped on the curbside.

Martha's feet turned to stone. She had been so preoccupied with finding the address and finding the house that she'd forgotten to prepare anything to say to Olive's mother. She'd forgotten that she'd have to explain her unusual gift. Nothing came to her. She hoped that somehow the right words would automatically flow from her mouth at the proper time.

Which door to go to? Side or front? And what to call her? Mrs. Barstow? Ms. Barstow? Olive's mother?

It felt to Martha as though a bird were inside her, beating its wings.

"You lost?"

Martha looked up. The thin voice belonged to an old man coming around the side of the house from the backyard. He walked with a slight limp.

"You lost?" he asked again when he was

within a few feet of her. He had a raw complexion and sunken cheeks. His cloudy eyes were rimmed in red. What little hair he had was white and wispy, like cobwebs pasted around his ears.

"Is this where Olive Barstow lived?" Martha managed to say, trying to overcome her sudden bashfulness and trying to be polite.

"She passed on, you know," said the man. "A shame."

"Yes," Martha said, lowering her head. The thought crossed her mind that the man was Olive's grandfather. She raised her head again. Their eyes met. "But is this where her mother lives? I'd like to give her something."

"Used to live here. Gone now. She moved out last week. See?" He waved an arm at the collection of garbage and frowned. "Good thing garbage day is tomorrow."

"Do you know where she moved?" Perhaps her new house was just a bike ride away.

"No. She talked about going to Oregon or Washington. I think that's where she's from. One or the other. Who knows?" The old man pulled a handkerchief from his front pants pocket and wiped his forehead. Before he replaced it, he folded the handkerchief into a perfect square. "Kind of a different woman. Lots of ups and downs. Either she didn't talk at all—almost unfriendly. Or else she talked endlessly—blah, blah, blah—about nothing."

"Oh," said Martha. She looked at the jar. Because the sun was penetrating it, streaks of refracted light marked her palm.

The old man extended his hand. "I'm John," he told her. "Mr. Waverly."

"I'm Olive," Martha said distractedly. After a beat or two, her entire face reddened. "I mean, I'm *Martha*." Her voice cracked. "My name is *Martha*." She grabbed his hand weakly, shaking her head.

"It's hot. I need to sit." John Waverly let himself down slowly onto the top concrete step and motioned for Martha to join him.

She sat on the bottom step.

"Did you know Olive?" he asked.

"Not really."

"I didn't think so. At least, I never saw you here. Never saw *any* kids, for that matter. I'm the landlord. I live downstairs. Olive and her mother lived upstairs. Never saw her play with other kids. Not once. She was always alone.

She'd sit right here," he said, patting the top step, "writing away in one of her notebooks. I'd see her ride her bike sometimes, but always with a notebook, always alone. She was kind of an odd thing. Lonely Little Olive Pit, I called her. Not to her face, of course." He paused. "No father in the picture either," he added, as though he had just remembered this piece of information, a footnote.

It made Martha uncomfortable to hear these comments. For some reason, John Waverly's words were like a pin to her heart.

He rubbed his chin reflectively. "I'm haunted by that girl."

Me, too, thought Martha.

John Waverly tipped his head back and sniffed the air like a dog. "Hot," he said. "Hot, hot, hot." He sighed. "Well, I'm going in to the air-conditioning. Stay as long as you like. And if you drink all your water," he continued, nodding at Olive's ocean, "feel free to take a refill with my hose. It's around the side. You should have a bigger water bottle on a hot day like this. You'll empty that tiny thing of yours in one gulp."

John Waverly rose unsteadily from the step,

dipping once before making it all the way up, limped along the sidewalk, and disappeared into the house.

Martha had thought she'd be making a kind of permanent connection to Olive, and now felt unmoored. She had never considered that Olive's mother would have moved, or moved so far away.

Olive sat right here, thought Martha. Right on this very spot. She got up to leave. She walked over to the garbage. It wasn't really a decision, more an impulse. Among the stained sofa cushions and broken chairs and brittle houseplants and moldy shower curtain, Martha saw a plastic bucket crammed with paintbrushes. She plucked a brush from the middle of the bunch. It was the thinnest one, and longest. Its bristles were stiff and well used.

Instinctively Martha went back to the concrete steps. She knelt down, took a deep breath, and blew at the top step, clearing away the dirt and small debris. Then she opened the little jar of seawater. It smelled fishy. She waited, breathing softly, working at the bristles with her fingers to loosen them. Finally she dipped the brush into the jar of water and wrote Olive's name on the top step. Martha retraced the letters until the jar was empty. She watched intently—the concrete turned dark and then light again as the water evaporated. Olive's name was there one moment, then gone the next, like a flicker in the great scheme of things.

"Good-bye," she whispered.

Martha gently placed the empty jar and the brush into one of the garbage cans as she left.

Good-bye.

Hearing about Olive and her mother from John Waverly had made Martha sad and frightened her a bit. Olive was brave, she thought. Braver than I am.

If I met you now, I would be your friend, Olive. Martha repeated the sentence in her mind, hoping the message would somehow be received.

The neighborhood was quiet and still, except for the sleepy drone of air conditioners, one passing car, and the *psst, psst, psst* of a lone sprinkler. Martha meandered a few blocks out of the way to lengthen the short walk home. She turned right, then left, then right again, weaving through the streets.

She pretended she was walking along the beach at Godbee's—a silly daydream—first with Olive and Tate, then alone. Suddenly she began to run—pretending to be running in and out of the breaking waves, and then straight out to the horizon, right on top of the water.

Her sandals slapped against her heels. Her shadow looked like a smooth machine.

She'd only run a short distance when she realized that what she wanted was to be home. She turned at the next corner to take the fastest way. Within minutes, she was in her own yard.

After catching her breath, she opened the front door and stepped into the familiar light of the entryway. Everything was safe here, stamped on her heart: the noises, the smells, the look and feel of each room. And even though she hadn't gone far or been gone long, she needed to say it, for her own sake, and she did so, loudly: "I'm home."